BOOK OF EXEMPLARY WOMEN

BOOK OF EXEMPLARY WOMEN

STORIES

DIANA XIN

YESYES BOOKS | PORTLAND

COVER AND INTERIOR DESIGN: ALBAN FISCHER
PROJECT LEAD: KMA SULLIVAN
AUTHOR PHOTO: DEVIN MUÑOZ

ISBN: 978-1-946303-09-7
PRINTED IN THE UNITED STATES OF AMERICA

PUBLISHED BY YESYES BOOKS
1631 NE BROADWAY ST #121
PORTLAND, OR 97232
YESYESBOOKS.COM

KMA SULLIVAN, PUBLISHER
KARAH KEMMERLY, MANAGING EDITOR
GALE MARIE THOMPSON, SENIOR EDITOR
ALBAN FISCHER, GRAPHIC DESIGN
JILL KOLONGOWSKI, MANUSCRIPT COPY EDITOR
JAMES SULLIVAN, ASSISTANT EDITOR

For my mother and sister,
formidable women both.

CONTENTS

HERE'S THE CHURCH, HERE'S THE STEEPLE

At 23, she became a pastor's wife. They held a small ceremony at the church where he was minister. It would take him four more years of seminary to become pastor, but that was the general idea. Her bridesmaids were two friends from college. One of them said: "I'm so jealous I could murder you." The other said: "Please don't kill yourself. Call me. If you're ever thinking about it."

*

The first ten days of her marriage, she did not have a single bowel movement. She told her husband travel made her bloated. They had only gone to California.

On the last day of their honeymoon, she sighed with relief in the corner stall of an In-N-Out as one tremendous shit began to stretch her rectum.

Her husband was eating a burger when she came out. "Ready to go?" he asked with a smile and a dot of orange mayo on his chin. "Yes," she said. "We'd better get to the airport."

*

The anticipation of sex had been exciting, but the act of sex itself was boring, until it became extremely exciting, for about six months, and then went back to boring. He liked for her to get him hard with her mouth and her hand. This was, perhaps, most boring. Running her hand up and down his penis, she would hold it erect and think of the old children's rhyme: *Here's the church, and here's the steeple. Open my legs, and Lord make some people.*

They had sex for the purpose of procreation, and they met with great success. Three boys in five years. Every prayer was a prayer for sleep.

*

The head pastor at the church where her husband became associate pastor had a wife. Let's call her Betty Do-Better. Betty had a calling, too, which was to help her find her calling. She had no musical talent and was asked to leave the choir. The luncheon dishes she prepared were deemed watery and bland, unsuitable for children. When her Christmas pageant rehearsal veered into a discussion around the stages of labor, she was removed from the roster of Sunday School teachers.

After she let slip that she once wrote for her college paper, Betty issued a church newsletter. When babies arrived, she wrote birth announcements. When illness arrived, she wrote prayer requests. When the Internet arrived, she wrote code for a church website.

When boredom arrived, she wrote obituaries for Betty:

Fell off the church roof while cleaning bird shit from the steeple.

It was as if the tornado had honed in for her cochlear hairdo.

The killer bees could not resist her saccharine exterior.

*

She once attended the funeral of a young woman she didn't know, and she cried so hard people began to look at her with annoyance and suspicion. The woman had been killed by a drunk driver. Her husband knew the parents. She tried to contain herself, but that only exacerbated the situation as each sob then tore out of her throat at unpredictable points with a wrenching bray.

The kinder guests approached her afterward and asked cautiously how she knew the deceased. She could only shake her head and shrug, sometimes with a hiccup.

Back home, her husband asked, for perhaps the only time in their marriage, if she was doing quite all right. It wasn't that he didn't care. It was just that he was careless.

She was fine, she said, a little dehydrated but refreshed after all that sobbing, which then made her feel guilty for disrespecting the parents' grief and taking advantage of the daughter's death.

*

She did not cry at her mother's funeral. She was fourteen years old. She had forgotten how to cry. During her teens, she would chop onions just so she could sit on the kitchen floor and contemplate sorrow. After each session, she would pray for the forgiveness of her sins and ask to become a good person. A woman with virtue, like her mother. Years later, she still waited for an answer.

*

The biggest heat wave in 72 years. They were driving down Highway 55 to get to a wedding, three sweaty sons stuffed into the backseat of the Camry. She turned to her husband. "Can't you do something about this?"

He shook his head sadly. "I'm just a man. I don't control the weather."

"I was talking about the air conditioner."

Shortly after her 35th birthday, she stopped believing in God and began writing erotica. She read somewhere — Good Housekeeping? — that women reached their sexual peak at age 40. For once, she felt ahead of the curve. She used the pen name Greenleigh Ardour, and never posted a photo. This only boosted her success. It lent her mystique.

After her fourth book — a paranormal-historical about a jewel thief who is tracked down by a detective whom she then learns is a vampire while she herself is the third reincarnation of the vampire's mortal lover — a website called Nymphs in Peril asked for an interview. She agreed, and they sent a list of questions to her secret e-mail alias.

Question number 5: *What is the key to good sex?*

She answered, Prayer.

Can you expand on that?

Everything we do is an act of prayer. The act of living demands an act of praying — even if you do not know to whom you are praying, even if you do not believe in praying. The summation of our human desires and yearning culminates in the act of prayer and promulgates in the act of sex. Therefore, good sex requires devout prayer.

The paranormal-historical received an award from the Erotica Readers & Writers Association, in the category of short-length ebooks. She asked that an administrator accept the award in her place and that the statue be delivered to her P.O. box.

Later, when her writing took off in new directions — a woman who loved a falcon, a woman who loved the taste of dirt, a woman who loved nothing because she had a prosthetic heart — she lost most of her fan base. She continued writing.

The object of her first seduction was a handsome mustachioed man with studs in his ears and a Chinese character tattoo on his forearm.

"It means faith," he said, after they shared two shots of Jameson at a bar on the outskirts of Urbana-Champaign, about four miles from the university campus hosting the Sisters in Christ retreat.

"In what do you place your faith?" she asked, tracing the slashes of black ink on his skin.

For once in her life, she wanted to be a plot twist. In her mind, a seedy motel room was inevitable. But after throwing down his credit card, he thanked her for the good time and called her ma'am.

As in, you take care now. As in, try your hand elsewhere.

During the next 48 hours of worship, prayer, and Bible-assisted therapy, his words rankled inside her, a twist with no release. Twice, she excused herself from small group discussion to go masturbate in a bathroom stall.

*

The woman who loved the falcon could not say why she loved the falcon, except perhaps that in her life there had always been this falcon. When they were young, she would grind worms to meal in her mouth and deliver the pulp into the yawning beak. When the hawk missed the hunt, she took a knife and cut open her abdomen to expose her entrails to its predatory gaze. But the falcon, bound to natural instinct, took pleasure only in its escape back to the wild, wherein, unpracticed in pursuit and myopic due to customary hooding, it stumbled and starved and continued pushing toward the precipice.

*

Because of her marital position in the church, women she did not consider her friends would take her into their confidence. This never ceased to surprise her. She carefully coined her advice: *The best part of prayer is a little more Jesus in your cup. A family is forever. There's probably a psalm for that.*

When the wife of her lover approached her for counsel on reinvigorating a marriage, she made an attempt at honesty: "Forget him. His jokes are lame and his body is sagging. You have to find your own happiness."

She followed through on her own advice. The only thing she missed was the smell of his aftershave lingering like a guest at her kitchen table.

*

The woman who loved the taste of dirt could no longer eat the dirt because she developed a deathly food allergy. Instead she smeared the dirt over her skin, smelled it on her fingertips, packed it into her ears.

She craved the dirt so much she forgot what she was craving. Her life was one long and undefined craving. Finally—at the risk of anaphylaxis, blindness, even death—she ate the dirt—rapaciously, achingly, lovingly—but it no longer tasted the way she remembered.

*

Church picnic in July. Floral prints and sun hats, children catching grass stains, a pig on a spit. A fly landed on her plate and rubbed its pulvilli over her potatoes. Her husband droned on beside her and his voice, the humidity, or the quantity of food ingested—all of it weighed down on her until she struggled to breathe. The sky was dense and heavy, pushing down against them. The blades of grass leaned into the heat, their stalks still and eager to break. The afternoon darkened as it plodded on, and soon the wail of tornado sirens echoed down the streets.

Wind rattled house rattled windows. Her youngest, the one still at home, sat in the basement playing Solitaire on his laptop, his screen glowing in the darkness. She went upstairs to collect candles and stopped in front of the bathroom window, remembering how one could climb out of it and onto the roof. All day, she had wanted a breath of fresh air. She bunched her nightgown in her fist to keep it from billowing. The wind wrapped around her like the current of a warm river, every drop of it roaring.

She raised her arms in surrender, as if to say: *Come. Come get me. Take me away from here. Swallow me. Let me be a part of you.*

She imagined the sky opening, a hand descending to snatch her in its fist. But the wind carried on and away. The tornado never bothered to show up.

*

When the head pastor retired, the duties of planning the farewell parties fell upon the wife of the associate pastor, the next head pastor. This was, in fact, still her. During dinner, she imagined slamming a plate over every guest's head. Stun them out of talking so they'd keep the inane drivel inside. For the retired pastor's bald dome, slops of mushroom gravy. His wife's tinsel blonde perm smeared with gelatinous berries, a pouf of cream near the top.

Hours after everyone left, she walked around the block in her nightgown, trying to curb insomnia. When that didn't work, she went into the kitchen and brought all their plates into the yard. The ones she had just cleaned as well as the ones in the back of their cabinets. It took several trips. The china with the pink rosebuds. The china with the fruit cornucopias. The heavy porcelain with the embossed grapes. After the plates were in three neat stacks, she stood on the sidewalk and hurled them at the house like the Olympic javelin thrower she never was. What an arm she had.

The sound of plates shattering sent shivers down her spine and brought her husband outside. He begged her to come back in. She complied but only to get away from the neighbors' leering eyes.

They sat together in the kitchen, drinking peppermint tea.

"Do you have a brain tumor?" he asked. "Is that why you're acting like this?"

"No," she said. "I'm sick of these plates."

He was silent. "But you picked them out yourself."

She shook her head. "I'm not sick of the plates. I'm sick of this life. This is not the life I want anymore."

They considered what this meant.

Finally, he said, "I wish you had a brain tumor."

And his face was so lost, so forlorn, that she could almost see the young man in him again, abandoned and betrayed somewhere inside this defeated, hypertensive, trustworthy pastor he'd grown into. He'd spent his life equipping himself to confront illness and death and other people's pain. She wondered if this occluded him from his own life. There was nothing she could do to change this or to comfort him, so she took his hand in hers and kissed his knuckles, their ridges strange and cracked like land she never knew.

*

The woman with a prosthetic heart preferred the new mechanical organ, its steady tick over the irregular thumps prone to random bursts of passion. It was not that she had never loved. She had, in fact, loved fiercely and longed for love in return, so much that it exhausted all her resources. Now she lived a quiet, staid life, in a house with many hallways, each one lined with doors she never bothered to open. Sometimes she would hear a distant knocking and tilt her head to listen, trying to determine where and what might be stirring. She knew better than to search out a thing that wants your attention, but one night that sound kept getting louder, that dead thing kept pounding. At the end of the hallway was a line of light, glowing bright beneath the door. She gazed down her shadow and watched it grow shorter and shorter until she got close enough to grasp hold of the cold brass doorknob. She flung open the door, and behold! What did she expect to find? Her long-lost heart? A breath of air? It was just another room, clots of dust in the corner. Maybe it was a closet, or a place to hide the furnace.

THE MAGNIFICENT FUNERALS OF GRAND AUNTIE DU

Grand Auntie Du passed away in her sleep on a bright April morning when the neighbor's boy was parking his bike over her hyacinths and the live-in nurse was humming to Cat Stevens downstairs. The last breath sighed past her chapped lips. A ladybug crawling along the wall opened its wings and lighted on the window screen. The blue curtains rustled in the breeze as death waited for the nurse to come discover it.

Oooh, baby, baby, it's a wild world, sang Cat Stevens and the nurse, *and I'll always remember you like a child, girl.*

On the day of the funeral a week later, Mr. Chang returned from his trip to Taiwan and, upon receiving the news of the death, grabbed Grand Auntie Du's will from his office before driving to the Lius' house.

Mrs. Liu was preparing at least three hundred green tea mochi bean paste rice cakes for the reception that evening. Grand Auntie Du was one of the most long-standing elders of the New Chinese Southern Baptist Church of Seattle, and Mrs. Liu knew the attendance level would be unmatched. As one of Grand Auntie Du's closest caregivers, nearly considered her surrogate daughter, Mrs.

Liu had many duties for the funeral but even so, she washed the flour off her hands and pared an apple for the lawyer.

Mr. Chang spread his papers over the coffee table. "There," he said, his finger falling into the sea of words.

She squinted. *Item 5.14: To perform in a fiduciary capacity in making any and all decisions or elections as pertains to the passing, haunting, and consoling of my dear ghost, whom I bequeath upon my expiration.*

"But what do you mean by a ghost?"

"She was very adamant about it." Mr. Chang pushed his bifocals up the bridge of his nose. "She said it followed her all the way over from China."

Mr. Chang had handled Grand Auntie Du's will since she was first diagnosed with stomach cancer fourteen months ago. After four revisions and five calls in the night, he had quelled his habit for logic and obediently penned it all down. In January, he went to the hospital as requested and read it out loud to Grand Auntie Du. She was very satisfied, Grand Auntie Du had said, to tie up loose ends. Her stomach, once empty for years, was now full of cancer, and better to die on a full stomach than an empty one. Actually, she would rather not die at all, but so be it. Not even a gold chamber pot could save a king. Before Mr. Chang left for his golf game, she reminded him once more about the ghost, for he had been the most bothersome of all her possessions.

"I don't remember she ever mentioned any ghost before," Mrs. Liu said. "Did she say who it was?"

"That I would not know," Mr. Chang said dryly. "She also left you a collection of teacups, a few pieces of jade, and some porcelain. Also, an old book. Those might be worth something, with the right market."

"Yes, of course, the book was her father's. The only one in his library that wasn't burned. Have some more fruit, please."

"Would you like to see the rest of the list?"

Mrs. Liu took the documents from him. "How did she ever have so many things?"

"The rest is mostly junk, and the house was already his daughter's. She wants to take possession as soon as possible."

"We'll need to find somewhere to store all this."

"Or haul it down to the Goodwill. They'll sort you out."

"I just hope there's someone we can pass the ghost to."

Mr. Chang chuckled and bit into a slice of apple. Before he could grab another slice, Mrs. Liu showed him out so she could continue setting up for the day. She had never much liked the man anyway.

The congregation of the New Chinese Baptist Church of Seattle picked out the best outfits they had in black and navy, practicing somber expressions in the mirror as they dressed. The most devout members, of whom were Mrs. Choi and Mrs. Harvey, directed the kitchen staff in cooking great vats of fried noodles and macaroni, to be served following the funeral.

Michelle, the twelve-year-old daughter of Mrs. Liu, rubbed her eraser against her notebook until the paper wrinkled. She rubbed out four lines from the end of her poem and swept the eraser bits into her bed.

Uncle Moy, now the eldest member of the congregation after Grand Auntie Du's death, poked his granddaughter's hairpin into his earwax.

Pastor Rickens flipped through his Bible and jumped up to run another comb through his hair. It was his first funeral service with this congregation.

Auntie Emmie called Mrs. Liu to say she had found a monk.

The ghost in Grand Auntie Du's basement wept miserably, for it had been a week since he had any company.

Inside the casket that smelled of pine and formaldehyde, Grand Auntie Du blinked.

On the seventh day, the *hun* returned, and Grand Auntie Du rose from her body and her casket, the polished wood passing through her quite smoothly, though it was a bit cold. She squeezed her way out the parlor through a keyhole and blinked in the sunlight. She did not remember it being so bright.

The sidewalks glittered and she followed them forward, crouching at the jarring screech of cars. It had been so very quiet for so long. She found her way home despite there being no signs to welcome her and no talcum powder spread on the floor to catch her footprints. She flung open the doors to her basement and Ghost looked up, an iridescent tear dangling off the edge of his nose.

I have the most tiresome song in my head, Ghost, Grand Auntie Du declared. *My, look how dusty you've become.*

She swept the cobwebs off his shoulders as he rubbed strings of sticky tears from his eyes.

You must look your best at my funeral, Ghost. It shall be my only one. How considerate of them to hold it today.

But Ghost did not wish to leave Grand Auntie Du's basement.

You must come, Ghost, Grand Auntie Du frowned. *Or who shall I sit with? And if you do not leave the basement today, you will have to anyway once the new people move in for they will not like you as I do. You are much too shy and you never practice your English.*

She grabbed his hand and pulled him along.

*

It was magnificent weather for a funeral. A blanket of clouds had moved across the sun so that the sky was neither offensively blue nor lugubriously gray, but a soft overcast pearl, like the wings of a dove. Far beneath, the pink petals of newly emerged cherry blossoms fluttered against the green gills of their buds. The earth still smelled of recent rain.

The guests took their seats and folded their hands, waiting for Pastor Rickens to begin. Grand Auntie Du sat perched on a tree branch with Ghost at her side, peering past the pale blooms in excitement.

The choir sent chilling notes into the breeze, and no one was flat. Lizzie Gam had lost her voice at a basketball game, so was resigned to lip syncing. Pastor Rickens began his message and he did not spit once, his mouth dry from drugstore antihistamines.

"And though we are most grieved by the departure of our dear sister," Pastor Rickens paused as the translator interpreted. "We rejoice that she has returned home ... our dear Father in heaven who welcomes her with open arms ... she who has overcome the temptations of this world, the greed of man, the evils of communism ... may she rest forever in peace, Amen."

Grand Auntie Du smiled broadly.

It is a pity you cannot go there, Ghost. She patted his knee.

The eulogies began and she turned her attention to little Michelle.

Michelle tripped through the first few lines of her poem, the paper shaking in her hands. She hoped no one would mind too much that "time" and "shine" did not really rhyme. Her voice grew clearer as she went on, "And though she has returned home to the Lord, I'll always remember her whom I adored."

Grand Auntie Du clapped her hands soundlessly.

What a wonderful poet she'll be. You will like her, Ghost. I've left you with the Lius, so you must make yourself pleasant to them. Oh, but it was a lovely poem, was it not? Though now I've got that horrid song in my head again.

Auntie Emmie was at the podium next, recounting bits of Grand Auntie Du's tumultuous life fleeing from China to Hong Kong to the U.S. and then remembering her greatest recipes.

It's not just my pork bao. My shrimp dumplings are also better than hers.

Grand Auntie Du was quite bashful to have received so many compliments, though she wondered why no one had mentioned her exceptional salted fish porridge. She had prepared it every year to be served after Christmas Eve service. Pastor Rickens closed the ceremony with a prayer and the guests rose from their seats, greeting each other as they left for the reception at the church.

"She was such a pious woman," Pastor Rickens said to Mrs. Liu. "So faithful in her suffering."

Mrs. Liu glanced at Auntie Emmie, who was shouting into Uncle Moy's left ear about the benefits of fish oil.

A group of uncles discussed the best medical insurance providers and a cluster of aunties made plans for the sisters' retreat.

Several of them congratulated Michelle on her beautiful poem. Her knees still trembling, Michelle felt as if some new gift of power was speeding through her and everything she saw could be spun into literature like straw into gold. She studied the crumbling gray headstones and decided she would write a poem for every dead body underneath them. And one day the poems would be collected into a hardcover book and dedicated to the Lake View Cemetery. The residents of.

But then it struck her that the book would be disloyal to Grand Auntie Du. Hers would no longer be the only poem and then it would not matter. It would not have any importance at all. For a moment, Michelle thought she could smell Grand Auntie Du in the air, the medicinal ginseng softened by a twang of oranges, and it felt as if *that*—the strange whiff of wind that sank down to her stomach before hurrying away—was really what death meant, and she had misunderstood it all along.

Grand Auntie Du followed her guests back to church and watched as the hallway filled to capacity. She had grown quite adjusted to the world again and it was delightful to soak in the noise and hubbub as little children scampered through her legs. But Ghost, who did not like people in large quantities, wondered if it was perhaps time to head for heaven.

Not yet, Ghost. We have much to do. And perhaps heaven will not be my home after all. Grand Auntie Du smiled slyly as she spotted Mrs. Liu.

Mrs. Liu picked up a few used dishes and tossed them into the garbage. This was all she could do to help with the cleaning. She could not stay. She had a monk to meet. This was Grand Auntie Du's request. Dodging Pastor Rickens, for she did not want to incite his consternation, she ushered Michelle toward the exit.

Knowing the impressionable nature of her daughter, Mrs. Liu dropped Michelle off at the library before heading home. She didn't want to risk leading her astray in her faith.

With Auntie Emmie's help, Mrs. Liu cleared off the coffee table to make room for the altar. Wiping clean a framed photograph of Grand Auntie Du, they placed her at the very center. Then they planted sticks of red incense into an old flowerpot and prepared a plate of fruit for the offering.

Don't I look young, Ghost? Grand Auntie Du admired the old photo. *I was thirty then. It was my first day in America. Or, no, you're quite right, we were twenty-three. Our final days in China. That jade in my necklace was a gift from my dear Kunshan. You remember him? But poor Kunshan did not go to heaven, either. We didn't know about heaven then. Richard will be there, of course. I was married a long time to Richard. What a nice man he was. But oh, my poor dear Kunshan.*

In the last months of her life, she had wondered if, maybe, she would run into him again in her death, if maybe he would even be there, to lead her through the transition. Now she was grateful she had not shared that silly hope with anyone else.

She jumped at a loud screech from outside.

The monk pulled into the driveway in his silver Lexus. "Sorry I'm late, I had to borrow a robe," he said at the door. "It's always better with the robe. I forgot to ask on the phone, but you don't got any cats, do you? I'm allergic."

Mrs. Liu welcomed him inside and showed him to the bathroom where he could change.

"Is he allowed to have hair?" she whispered to Auntie Emmie.

"I don't think it matters anymore," Auntie Emmie said, tossing sunflower seeds into her mouth. "Hair, no hair, all the same. The woman at the bakery said he's excellent. He lived five years in a temple in Xi'an where they didn't even get tofu."

"I don't mind the hair," Mrs. Liu said. "There's just so much of it."

The monk came out swathed in a maroon robe. A yellow cloth hung off his shoulder and ran diagonally across his torso until it tied at his waist. His narrow face looked smaller than before, between robe and hair. Thick and a tad wavy, his hair was cut in a manner so that the middle stuck up more than the rest, in a boxy way that reminded Mrs. Liu of a hedge. He smiled at the women, displaying an uneven row of yellow teeth that once did not touch tofu for five years. The freckled skin around his eyes wrinkled.

"I'll just sit here, do my chanting," he said, pulling out a string of brown beads from the side of his robe. "Could I get a glass of water or something? If it's purified. You wanted three hours, right? You got anything else planned? Music? Crying? Some people like it very traditional. I got some buddies who'll cry for you on short notice. They really bring the emotion, these guys. One of them's got a degree in theater."

"I think a few prayers should do fine." Mrs. Liu glanced at Auntie Emmie for confirmation. "Do most people still include the crying?"

"Well, it all depends," the monk said. "If they like the ceremony they'll do it, but it's all for show, you know? Always was. Hard to fit it all in these days, though. Even in China. No one has time for a proper death anymore."

Mrs. Liu lit the incense and the monk began, chanting as he rotated the beads around his hand, one by one. His voice grew low and sonorous. Mrs. Liu turned to Auntie Emmie and nodded with approval.

Swirls of incense filled the room and distorted the monk's words. His prayers rolled out like waves of the ocean and muted thunder.

Grand Auntie Du yawned.

Ghost gave her a mutinous look but Grand Auntie Du refused to consider him.

This is just in case I don't like heaven. We must always explore our options, Ghost, lest we get stuck in a muck of our own making. Oh, don't be a snob. Besides, it is nice to enjoy one's culture. Now pay attention, Ghost. You are being very rude.

Grand Auntie Du looked down demurely as she received her benedictions. When she awoke, the monk was already at the door, wearing a blue polo and slacks.

"You know," he said to Mrs. Liu, "you're supposed to have prayers every seven days, actually. It makes things easier. For the dead, I mean. I can come back next week, if you'd like, and I do the seventh for free. It helps make for a better reincarnation. Protection against the dung beetle, you know?"

"This will have to be it for us, I'm afraid. It's really just ... a courtesy."

"Right-o then. Thought I'd check. That's what's wrong with Buddhists today, though. There's no more fear of the dung beetle. Here's my business card anyway. I'm at the dealership up near Boren."

"You sell cars?"

"It's a hard livelihood for monks these days," he said. "Good luck with everything now. Sorry for your loss."

"Thank you for your prayers." Mrs. Liu held the door for him.

"I can tune a piano, too, by the way," he said. "You gotta tune them in the spring after all that wet season."

She wondered if she should get Michelle piano lessons again, watching the sad slope of his shoulders as he walked toward the shiny car.

Grand Auntie Du waved goodbye to the monk from the window before turning to Ghost, who had grown quite peevish.

I suppose we can only wait now, she said. I think I should enjoy heaven, Ghost, but there is so much I can do if I were to live again. I could visit the museum in France, or learn to ski. Perhaps I could have children in my next life. I would have been a good mother, don't you agree? And maybe...

She fell quiet. When she was young, her best friend had the misfortune of falling in love with a poor man. Her parents refused to let them marry, so they had exchanged a promise, one that was common among young lovers of that time. They swore they would be together in the next life no matter what, even if they had to be horses or cows. But she and Kunshan had never entertained such foolishness.

Ghost patted her shoulder. She mustered a smile for him.

She had been lucky, after all. Her first marriage was never consummated, the second was better to forget, but the third had served her very well. She'd remained fond of dear Richard up till the day he died. She'd kept her promises as a wife.

They watched as Mrs. Liu came over, reaching through them to open the window. She waved at the incense to clear the air and offered Auntie Emmie a slice of pear from the altar.

I should not like to catch cancer again. Grand Auntie Du shook her head. Dying is a ghastly affair and it is preferable to do it only once.

She reached out to feel her stomach where the cancer had lumped into tumors and clawed through her organs.

Ghost! Ghost! My stomach is missing!

She wiggled her fingers in the gaping hole of her abdomen. The doctors had removed three-fourths of her stomach a year ago, but she had never had a hole.

This is very peculiar.

The two of them retraced their steps, walking back towards the church to see where Grand Auntie Du had misplaced her stomach. The sun was setting and it washed the sky in red.

Halfway there, she stubbed her foot against a fire hydrant and her pinky toe rolled into the street.

They hurried onward and rushed into the sanctuary, hoping to find help. The pews were empty but Grand Auntie Du stepped forward anyway and peered around the altar for the door to heaven. As she seemed to be falling apart, she thought it would be wise to leave, rather than wait for reincarnation. The Chinese were rarely punctual.

She knelt before the cross, but no stream of light flooded down upon her. She held her breath, and her lungs shriveled until they were loose and waving in the air like empty sacks. Still she waited patiently and bade Ghost to keep watch. The red in the sky deepened to a purple bruise and soon it was night.

Didn't I say how important it is to explore other options? Especially in such matters as the afterlife.

Afraid that the Chinese gods would not feel comfortable inside a church, Grand Auntie Du went back outside and sat in the parking lot. The wind was cold and birds rustled overhead. In the distance, cars chased shadows down the highway and above it all, she could still hear a familiar voice thrumming in the breeze, *Oh baby baby, it's a wild world....*

I wish that dreadful song would go away. I can hardly think for all the racket. I don't remember what I need to do anymore, Ghost, if I must drink the soup and forget my life or if I go to the judge first. Heaven at least had only one hell. But the Chinese decided to have nine. Perhaps they will be fast.

The wind picked up as they waited. Grand Auntie Du's remaining toes crumbled into dust and bits of leaves. Her fingers stiffened into long dry branches.

She tried to remember what she had once known. If she could

remember it, perhaps she would not be abandoned. A memory as distant as golden strands of wheat waving in the fields rose from the past and she could smell the singed air of China as if it were licking her on the neck. Her aunt appeared in the corner, kneeling in front of an open hearth as she fanned dried husks of corn into the fire to heat their millet porridge. She herself was a young girl, staring at the curious contrast of her aunt's tanned skin against the starched white cloth draped over her dress. Birth and death were stale in that morning breeze, and the wind stung of smoke and gunpowder. Her aunt was telling her about birth after death. Only half listening, she rolled a boiled egg along the wood slats of the table and felt the thin shell cracking against her palm. Her hands were small and smooth and the earth moved through them.

The baby's hands were even smaller. His fingertips were blue and so tiny but her mother had clipped the nails anyway. She had cut his hair as well and placed it all together in a black silk sachet. Beautiful hair, her aunt had said. It was dark and thick, a sign he had great inner *qi* and would have grown with vitality.

She'd woken in the middle of the night, stayed in her bed and tried not to listen. Something was wrong, she'd realized when the sun was rising, and she'd crept out into the courtyard. Her father carried the placenta in a washbasin to the storage room, where he removed three sacks of rice and flour from the corner and lifted a loose stone from the floor. She had watched curiously over his shoulder and peeked into the dark caverns of sifting dirt beneath the foundations of their house. Her father dropped the placenta into the darkness and said it would be safe there.

No matter how far one flew, the *hun* would always return and rejoin the placenta. The woman who taught English at the library told her this, not long after she had left that whole continent of land and arrived here. Maybe the woman was right.

Grand Auntie Du stood. *I must go and find my placenta, Ghost. Before it is too late.* —

Time was the essence of it all, and hers was running out. If time could collapse, then could space follow? Could she reach through the illusions of this world and grasp onto the next?

Somewhere my placenta is waiting for me, Ghost. She spoke with greater conviction than she had. *The house where we first lived, the geraniums by the front gate, but then the soldiers came . . .* —

A harsh gust of wind swept through and carried away Grand Auntie Du's liver. She stopped and mournfully watched it go.

Not long after the baby came, they had left the house behind and the placenta too. They'd headed south for a new start, the first of many.

If you can't go back, you can only go forward. Chin up, Ghost. We keep marching on. —

It was dark in the street and Grand Auntie Du narrowed her eyes to see. Her intestines, both large and small, unraveled as she hobbled along. They dangled behind her like the strings of a kite and stretched longer and longer as she walked on.

Which way shall we choose? she asked as they came up to the intersection. Ghost was silent, and when she turned to look for him, he was no longer there.

Ghost? Ghost!

But she was alone now, falling apart on a dark and unfamiliar street. Her heart jumped out of her chest as she started to run. Her intestines reached the end of their spool and fell limply to the ground, the kite sailing free. Rats skulked out from the cracks of the earth to sniff the air as Grand Auntie Du disappeared around the corner.

INTERMISSION

Every other Wednesday evening, the Northwest District Small Group of the Mendota Heights Church of the Holy Redeemer held a Bible study at one of the attendees' homes. Starting at six p.m., they would chat and eat a potluck dinner, sing praise, and then break for dessert before reconvening to study the Word. They found the dessert intermission best for digestion.

Most of the time, Jolie was excused on account of homework or some other clever reason—sore throat, important movie with important friends, emerging allergy to the mold problem at the Hatfield place. Tonight, however, it fell to Jolie's mother to host and there was no way out. She had to dust and clean and greet the guests and smile, displaying to everyone her exemplary behavior.

Leaning against the white pantry doors, she watched the adults flock around the kitchen island where the desserts were laid out. The snaps and falls of their conversation were something like the squawking of birds. "—I just can't stand the swearing in those movies—" "Can you believe those gas prices? They're *gas*-tronomical." George the Senior's horse-like laugh boiled up, and Jolie clenched her teeth. George the Junior smirked at her from across the room, wiggling his pinky in his ear.

And then her mother's voice. "Jolie, are you listening? Go get your poem. Show Reverend Stark what you wrote for class."

"Mom." Jolie rolled her eyes. She was thirteen in five months. She didn't need to do a show-and-tell.

"It's the most wonderful poem," her mother said.

"Jolie is very bright." The Reverend smiled at her in the way people smiled at little kids who thought they'd done something great, like coloring a giraffe purple. He had a smear of chocolate on his front tooth.

"It's too bad she's so shy." That was her mother's new excuse for why Jolie didn't go to Bible study, why she didn't talk to adults, and, now, why she didn't run and grab her poem.

But she wasn't shy. She was just sick of them, all these adults with their fake smiles, repeating their old, used lines.

The only one she could stand was Andria, who touched her on the shoulder. "Jolie, I haven't seen you in so long," she said in that sweet, breathy voice of hers, a hand resting on her swollen belly. "Come up to the bathroom with me. Let's freshen up."

When Jolie was younger and Andria, who lived down the street, was still her babysitter, Andria would powder Jolie's nose and paint her nails in a rainbow of colors, and Jolie would practice braiding Andria's beautiful blonde hair. Now Andria was married to Jack Sullivan who had bought the house next door and who did not believe in God. Jolie and her little sister Jessica had been the flower girls last August. Andria was going to have her own baby in just a few weeks. She said that Jolie would be her little boy's babysitter, and wasn't that perfect? It was a lot to take in, even for Jolie.

"So?" Andria said, leaning toward the mirror as she applied her lip gloss. "How do you like seventh grade? How are your classes?"

Jolie shrugged, studying her reflection next to Andria's. "Language Arts is all right."

She didn't know how Andria got her hair so soft and wavy.

Jolie's own hair was straight and stiff and boring brown. She was a long, bony twig standing next to Andria, who was lovely as a doll, only now she was cruelly overstuffed. She grew puffier each time Jolie saw her. Her belly was much bigger than a basketball. Jolie felt her face burn, remembering how she had once stuffed a basketball under her T-shirt.

"Is it exciting to be in a new school?"

"Not really. It's mostly boring."

Everything was supposed to be boring at almost-thirteen, it seemed. Everyone was always talking about being bored. It was never safe to say you liked a book or enjoyed talking to a boy or didn't mind a certain teacher.

Andria smiled at her. "You're so grown up," she said, and offered Jolie the lip gloss.

Jolie leaned toward the mirror, opening her mouth and moving the pink brush over her lips as Andria had done. Then she pressed her lips together and tasted the stickiness. There was no flavor or sweetness in it, only the vague smell of pencil shavings.

"Thanks." She handed back the lip-gloss.

Andria placed a hand over her belly. "Calm down now."

"Does it hurt?" Jolie asked. She watched as one side of the belly pitched forward.

"It's a bit bothersome, but he doesn't kick hard. He likes to move around. He's an active one."

But Jolie had meant the whole thing, what it was like to be pregnant. She could see Andria's belly button outlined behind her blue jersey dress.

"Do you want to feel him kick?"

Jolie shook her head. "No, thanks." She had touched a pregnant cat's belly once. She had cupped the shape of the kittens inside her palm. They were so strangely alive, squirming behind the thin, stretched-out skin. Jolie had worried she would squish them. Thinking about their slimy bodies, she'd pulled her hand away disgusted.

Back in the kitchen, the adults were scraping the last crumbs off their plates. Reverend Stark stood by the entrance to the living room, smiling at no one and clearing his throat to signal that it was time to get started. A few crumbs stuck to his argyle sweater vest at the place where his belly began to widen. Her mother said he was young, but Jolie wasn't so sure. He was beginning to go bald. Little white scales lined the pink skin near his temples. Finally, it was her mother who ushered the adults into the living room.

Alone now, Jolie surveyed the mess of chocolate-smeared dishes and half-eaten sweets. She ignored them all and selected an apple from the fridge, one with no bruises or blemishes. She rinsed it under the faucet and crunched into it, savoring the spray of juice.

She brought the apple down to the basement, where the kids were always banished. There had been a time when Jolie loved the basement nights. They filled the lower levels of everyone's house with games and noise. After her father died, those nights were the only time she could be herself without fear that her mother might be watching — or worse, that her mother was not watching but lying in bed, listening. She and Jessica had tiptoed around the house for months, afraid to watch television or play piano, afraid to talk above a whisper.

Downstairs, Jessica had already taken out Connect Four and Operation and Hungry Hungry Hippos, trying to interest the Hatfield twins and the Martin boy. They stared up at her blankly.

George the Junior lay sprawled on the bean bag chair, stuffing his face with another brownie. Chocolate streaked across his chin.

"So?" Jolie said. "What do you guys want to do?"

"I want to fart a candlestick on fire," said George the Junior. He laughed with his mouth wide open, revealing every bit of mashed brownie.

Jolie didn't know what had gone wrong with him. He was, after all, only one or two years younger than Jolie herself, but he acted worse than Jessica, who was nine.

"What about the rest of you?" Jolie asked.

The twin girls looked at her blankly and the little boy rubbed his nose. Jolie spotted the plastic white funny bone between his fingers and snatched it away. She dropped it back into the Operation box and closed the lid. "You can't give them little toys like that," she told Jessica. "They'll choke."

The little boy crumpled his face like he was thinking about crying. Jolie looked down at him sternly. "You'll choke."

"Let's play Hot Lava Monster," Jessica said.

"How?" They would need much more space to run across the room, and more people, too.

"We'll go in a circle and the little kids can sit in the middle. They can be lava the whole time, even if they tag us."

"I call beanbag for safety," George the Junior said.

They took the pillows and the couch cushions to set up more rocks, grabbing a plastic pink stool and dragging over the wooden toy chest. In the end, the circle was big enough, so they decided the little kids could move around but only if they crawled. The little kids were so excited to play a big-kid game, they didn't even mind being lava.

Jolie chose a sofa cushion as her safety, and each time someone shouted go, she skipped over to the next pillow and the next, until she made it all the way around. She was the tallest one with the longest legs, and she imagined herself jumping like a dancer. She even pointed her toes and added little scissor kicks. *Sissone! Pirouette!* she shouted the commands in her head. The kids shrieked with laughter and Jessica repeated her three-note giggle. George the Junior punctuated his jumps with shouts of "Take that!" and "Hallelujah!" Jolie was as quiet and light as a falling leaf, balancing one-legged on the pink stool. She could do this with an apple in her hand. Each time she reached safety, she took another bite.

The little kids actually managed to tag them a few times, but they didn't know to ask for any kind of reward. George the Junior kept adding more rules and tricks. One leg only, he'd say, or whoever got to safety last had to do the next run alone. When he was standing on her safety cushion and Jolie was only two rocks away, he turned without warning and came bounding back.

"Re-*verse*! Time to re-*verse*!"

Jessica turned the other direction, but Jolie, already in motion, couldn't react fast enough. George crashed into her. Her jaw snapped shut and she fell off the pink stool. She hit her arm against the toy chest, but that wasn't what hurt— George had struck her chest with his elbow. Pain reverberated from the center of her breast like ripples of red heat. Tears welled up in her eyes. George's legs were heavy across her stomach as he lay diagonally on top her.

She shoved him hard. "Get off me, you pervert." She had just learned the word, but it seemed like a word invented for George.

He rolled away and sat up, hugging his knees to his chest,

trying to hide his face even as he peered at her with sorry eyes. The little kids came over and huddled around her as well. They all saw her crying.

Jolie wiped the tears with the back of her hand. "Okay." She tried to keep her voice firm. "No more playing. We're watching a movie now. We're watching Toy Story."

No one argued, and that made her feel better. George hovered close to her as she stood up. She didn't want to look him in the face.

She started the movie and kept one light turned on so she could read Pride and Prejudice. The library book was so old the pages were yellow and she had to be careful turning them. Everyone in her class had chosen their own books for the Book Report in a Bag project, and Jolie had gotten permission to do Pride and Prejudice. It was a difficult book, like her teacher had warned her, and she couldn't concentrate with the movie playing. She gave up and went upstairs to use the bathroom. The adults were taking turns reading a Bible passage out loud as she crept by.

In the bathroom, she found streaks of russet brown on her underwear. She had been through this before, but it was still embarrassing. She had to take off her light khaki pants to check the back. There was no stain, and when she wiped, there was no blood, either. Her mother had said that she would get used to this, that she just had to count the days on the calendar, that it was easy. But womanhood made no sense at all. It was awful to wear a pad. They were itchy and smelled bad, like fish or old pennies. She went back to her room and grabbed a clean pair of underwear, then added a liner to be safe. The liners were more comfortable than the pads. Back in the bathroom, she gazed at herself in the mirror. This was her third period. Who knew how many more would come? Only if she were pregnant could she skip her period. She imagined the slither of half-formed bodies—all that was required to create a life.

"Gross," she said, making a face. The self in the mirror made a worse face. She shook her head to scatter the thoughts, and then she skipped downstairs.

Her mother was in the kitchen with Reverend Stark. Jolie stopped at the doorway, watching them. They stood too close together. The reverend murmured something she couldn't hear, but the soft, falling tones of his voice made her ears buzz. The back of her head burned. She watched as Reverend Stark lifted one beefy hand and placed a finger against her mother's cheek.

"Jolie." Her mother jumped back, away from the reverend. "What are you doing up here?"

Her voice was high and rushed. Jolie didn't answer. Reverend Stark looked at the two of them stupidly, his mouth half-open.

"How's everything downstairs?" Her mother wiped her fingers against the side of her pants.

"Fine." Jolie kept her face blank but refused to look away from her mother.

"What's everyone doing?"

"Watching."

"Oh, good." Her mother clasped her hands together, looking relieved, even though she despised TV. "Reverend Stark was just—" she paused, "explaining something. We better get back in there now."

They rushed to the living room. Her mother glanced back once, but said nothing. Jolie stood in the empty kitchen. Everything seemed different.

She was too hot. She did not want to go back downstairs. Outside, the night air was cold and sharp. She took several deep breaths until she felt the tightness inside her uncoiling. The moon was bright and full. It lit up the yard and the browned oak leaves caught in the grass. She walked over to the lilac bush and touched its bare branches, then to the raised garden bed her father had made for her mother, which was now filled with dirt, leaves, and shriveled weeds. Her mother had stopped gardening. There's just no time, she'd say. Jolie lifted a rock from the dirt just to hold its solid shape in her hand. Then she stood and looked up at the sky, where everything was still.

"What you looking for?"

Jack Sullivan was standing in his yard. His dog Cody, a black lab, trotted over and stuck his wet nose into one of the diamonds of the chain link fence. Jolie didn't know how long they had been there. She walked over to say hello to Cody, who was Andria's dog now, too. Jolie knew the dog better than she knew Jack Sullivan, who traveled for business.

He pointed a finger at her, eyes squinting. "Jessica. Right?"

"Jolie."

"I thought Jolie was the older one."

"I am the older one."

He slapped his forehead. "Right! Of course you are. Yep. I can see it now. You're definitely the older one."

She focused on patting the dog's snout. "Good boy, Cody."

"Jolie, Jolie, Jolie," he sang her name in a little melody. "So is that short for Jolene, or did they name you for Angelina?"

"It means beautiful," Jolie explained, embarrassed. "It's French. My dad spoke it."

Things shifted back into place inside of her. Reverend Stark didn't know how to speak French. He could never compare to her dad.

"A man of sophistication." Jack Sullivan smiled at her, or maybe it was a smirk. She glanced away and watched as Cody sniffed her hand. But then the dog lost interest and turned his nose to the side, sniffing *her*. Jolie took a step back and crossed her legs.

"So how's the party? How come you're not inside?"

Jolie looked up. "How come *you're* not at the party?" She tried to use the teasing lilt of that loud but pretty eighth grader, but it came out sounding more like her mother, unnecessarily stern.

He laughed though. "Doesn't seem like my kind of party." He nodded his head toward the living room window, and Jolie turned as well. Between the wheat-colored curtains, she could see the adults sitting in a circle. George the Senior was waving his hands in front of his face like he was swatting at butterflies.

"That's all pretend," Jolie said. "You should see what they do for real."

She didn't know why she had said that, but he leaned forward with interest, resting an elbow on the fence post. She had to go on. "They look like they're praying, but they're really incanting. Like, curses. To the devil."

"Oh, my." He peered toward the window. "Is that what they're doing?"

Jolie nodded. In Social Studies, they had acted out a scene from the Salem witch trials. Jolie had played one of the young girls in the courtroom.

"Revered Stark traffics with the devil." It felt good to say this.

Mr. Sullivan—Jack—shrugged. "I guess we all do, sometimes."

His eyes swept disinterestedly across the lawn.

"He drinks blood," Jolie went on. "Chicken blood."

Jack turned back to her, the corner of his lips twitching. "Chicken blood. That can't taste good."

The boldness that had raced through her dissipated as she grasped at what to say. "He likes it fine."

"Andria wanted some backyard chickens. Now I know why." He narrowed his eyes. "Are you out here trafficking with the devil, too?"

"No. Of course not."

"Maybe you should. You could tell some scary stories."

Jolie forced a smile, because he was expecting one. The dog ran off in pursuit of a squirrel or a rabbit, leaving her alone with Jack. She shifted her feet and pulled at a loose thread dangling from the hem of her shirt.

Jack lifted a hand to his head and stretched his neck. The inside of his arm was smooth and pale, unlike the outside, which was covered in coarse brown hair. As he stretched, his white T-shirt rose up, and Jolie could see another line of hair that trailed down his belly to the brass button on his jeans.

"So I married a blood-drinking Satanist," he said. "Now that is some tough news to swallow."

The adults stirred in the living room, getting up and rearranging the chairs. They wrapped up these evenings by praying out loud, sitting in groups of two or three.

"You won't tell Andria I said anything, will you?" she asked.

"Would they curse you if I did?" His eyes were amused, but she was serious now. "I'd hate it if they cursed you, on account of anything I did."

"Promise?"

"Cross my heart." He winked. "If you'll keep a secret for me."

A pack of cigarettes appeared in his hand. He held it out for her to see. Camels.

She shrugged. "I don't care if you smoke."

She knew her mother would disapprove—that she already disapproved. She thought Jack was irresponsible and too charming. H didn't pick up dog poop or keep up the front lawn. He was away from home far too often. If he came to church on Sundays and Bible study on Wednesdays, she'd be more charitable, but he hadn't and wouldn't.

Jack flicked his lighter and a small flame appeared. He shielded the flame and brought it up to the cigarette dangling from his mouth. Jolie watched as he closed his eyes and inhaled, then tilted his head and released a ghostly stream of smoke into the sky, which was much darker than before.

"I won't tell if you won't tell," she said.

"Sounds like we've got a deal."

He smoked his cigarette but no longer seemed to relish it. He took several puffs and then exhaled as if exasperated. A bird called out in the night. A cold breeze swept by and she hugged her arms around her chest. The button on his jeans glinted, the teeth of the zipper curving loosely around his crotch. She'd studied the diagrams in health class, the little pictures of the cartoon man facing the side. His penis, always a darker color than the rest of his skin, would dangle out like a spigot. The little elephant trunk, her friend had called it.

"So you think it's gonna snow soon?" he asked.

"What?" Her face flushed.

He was looking up at the sky. "Wondering when we're going to get snow. Got new skis this summer. Doesn't seem that cold yet." He held out a palm, like he was offering her something, but he was just testing the temperature. "You like snow?"

"It's okay," she said. "I like it all right."

"I love it," he said. "I was gonna do a trip to Colorado in January, but we'll see with Rosemary's baby on his way. Afton's okay, and I could go to Wisconsin, but I bet I could still make it to Denver. Just for a weekend. I've got buddies there."

"Sounds fun." She didn't know who he meant by Rosemary but she didn't want to let her confusion show.

"Hey. You'll be our babysitter, right? I'm glad. You're a pretty cool kid."

"Thanks." She didn't know what else to say. If she talked about her babysitting experience, she would only sound more childish. She wondered if she should check on the kids downstairs, but then Cody came running back to them, so she offered the dog her fingers to lick. His tongue was rough and warm.

Mr. Sullivan dropped the cigarette stub into the grass and stamped it out. He was still wearing summer flip-flops and tufts of hair curled along the top of his bare feet. He kicked away some loose dirt near the fence, making a shallow hole. He brushed the cigarette into the hole with his foot and covered it up again.

"All right now. I'm counting on you."

Jolie nodded. She knew it was just one of those adult jokes, that it wasn't serious. Still, she was sharing his secret.

"You won't rat me out?" The cigarettes were gone now and instead he was holding a pack of Doublemint gum.

"Attagirl." He held up his hand for a high five, like the gym teacher sometimes did, but this was different. She placed her palm carefully against his, making sure their fingers lined up. His hand was much bigger than hers. His skin felt calloused.

She hadn't realized how small her hands were. He could fold her hand entirely into his, but he didn't. They touched for only a moment.

"See you around, Jolie."

He turned to leave, whistling for Cody to follow. Jolie waited for his door to shut before going back in.

The adults had flocked into the kitchen. There was always more talking to be done, with the adults. They talked as they doled out leftovers, offering more of this and that, and then, "Please, we don't need any more sweets." They talked as they searched for their belongings—sweaters and shoes, purses and children. Across the room, Reverend Stark was finishing off the last piece of carrot cake. Cream cheese frosting stuck to the corner of his lips. He caught his thumb in his mouth and licked the frosting off. When he caught her gaze, he stopped and gave her a grimacing smile. She looked away. Her mother was in the foyer, saying goodbye to the Martins. George tapped her on the shoulder. "Sorry," he said, bowing his head several times. "Super sorry." Then he raced away to join his parents at the door.

Andria came down the stairs from the bathroom, keeping one hand on the railing and the other one against her back.

"How did it go?" she asked. "Did you have fun?"

Jolie shrugged, guilt dipping in her stomach. "We watched a movie." Andria nodded, as if she couldn't wait to hear more. "That was it," said Jolie.

"What movie did you watch?"

A wave of heavy exhaustion came over her. Was this nostalgia? It tired her to lie, but this was how the world worked, how it would always work from now on.

The house sank into a bright silence after everyone left. All the lights were still on. Jolie imagined what the house looked like from outside, from the yard, lit with emptiness.

"Better clean up," Jolie's mother said. Jessica was sent to tidy the basement, and then to bed. Jolie gathered the dirty dishes and sponged them in soapy hot water.

Her mother dried them with the green linen. "What do you think about Reverend Stark coming over sometime?" Her tone was careful. "For dinner, maybe."

Jolie paused. Her mind raced with mean things to say about his boring sermons, his gross way of guzzling down desserts. "Do we have to?" she asked.

"It'd be nice to have some company for dinner once in a while, don't you think?"

"No. I like it just the three of us."

"Oh."

The echo of her mother's voice reminded Jolie that a great sadness resided in her mother, and even when she was happy, a shadowy tendril could rise up and grip her throat or stomach. Maybe Jolie had inherited this, too, like her mother's nose or mouth, or maybe it was something everyone had, in different amounts. Either way, it was not something she could talk about. She rinsed the soap off another plate and handed it to her mother. "Tonight was fun," she said. "I'll go next time." That was all she could think to say.

Her mother's eyes shined triumphantly. "I knew you had fun at these. You act like you're so bored but what else are you going to do? Watch a movie by yourself? Now, that's boring."

Jolie rolled her eyes. But she would go next time. She would go every time if that was what she had to do to keep Reverend Stark away from her mother.

"Better go get ready," her mother said. "You've got school tomorrow. Thanks for helping."

Jolie moved quietly through her room so she wouldn't wake her sister, though she stopped to adjust the blanket that Jessica had nearly kicked off. She found her pajamas and brought them to the bathroom so she could change after she showered. She shut the bathroom door with a sense of relief. Brushing her teeth, she made faces in the mirror, Foaming Vampire and Rabid Dog. A pretty cool kid, he had said.

She glanced out the window. She couldn't see much but she knew the window faced the side of their house and their front lawn. Jolie paused, toothbrush still in hand. She rinsed and spat, swiping a handful of water across her mouth. The blinds were pulled up. If he were to look up from a cigarette or from the dog he was petting, there she would be in the window. He might even see her from inside the house. But they were in bed now. There was no one out there to see her.

Even so, she remembered the way his eyes lit up. Another secret to share. Slowly, standing in front of the mirror, she pulled her shirt over her head. The beat of her pulse was in her throat. She untied the drawstring at her waist, let the button loose and pulled the zipper down. Her khaki pants pooled around her ankles.

Her bra was dark navy blue. Padded A cups from Macy's. A pink rosette sewn onto white ribbon sat in the space between the two scoops. Her underwear was from the girls' section, patterned with pink hearts and yellow lightning bolts. Who decided that those things would go together? Pink and yellow. Hearts and lightning. She wondered if she was beautiful. She suspected not. Her chin was too long and her eyes too close together, but her collarbones looked nice. All collarbones looked nice.

Without taking her eyes away from the mirror, she reached behind her back and undid the clasp. Her skin tingled as she remembered the touch of his hand, but she did not look out the window toward his house. She did not look away from the mirror. She slid her thin arms through the straps of her bra, which she dropped to the ground.

Her boobs were so small. Just beginning to take shape. Breasts. Boobs. Neither one was the right word. She pressed the palm of her hand against the left one, giving it a light squeeze just to feel that familiar ache. Then she traced a lazy finger around the edges, the areola, like a man might, and gave it a pinch. The nipple rose up like the pink nose of some small animal. No, not pink. Something deeper than pink.

Jolie moved her palm up and down, the bud of her nipple an interruption against her skin. She held her breath. She did not look away from the mirror. If anyone saw her, they wouldn't be able to tell whether or not she was beautiful. She'd be too far away, just a figure in a window. But wouldn't they stop to watch?

A car alarm broke out somewhere down the street. Each blaring note grew louder and closer. In terror, she jumped into the tub, and pulled the shower curtain shut.

SOMEONE ELSE

And the zombie said, "Where is my head?"
— E OLIVA

The day Holly and Sean moved into their first home together, they found a dead animal left on the wooden slats of their back deck. It was unclear what kind of animal. The head was gone. The clump of gray fur was as long as Holly's forearm. It looked swollen, its insides spilling out from two long gashes, like a tomato that had burst. There was a tuft of a tail, they noted, and three paws, but there was no head.

"This is not good," Holly said. "This is a bad omen."

"Don't be ridiculous," Sean said. "This is nature."

He stood over the carcass (of a raccoon? a possum? what?), holding a shovel he had found in the shed. Nothing about this looked natural to Holly. He would have to pick up the carcass with the shovel and take it down the connecting stairs into the yard because they were on the second floor. And then what? Bury it in a hole? Dump it in the garbage can? They had no plastic bags. Everything was packed away.

"Don't bury it here," Holly said. "I want it gone. Take it away. Would you? Please?"

"How? I'm not walking down the alley with it."

"I don't know. I can't look at it anymore. I'm going to be sick if I keep looking at it."

She went back inside to unpack. After unloading a box of dishes, she looked out the glass panes of the storm door. Sean was digging a hole near the far end of the chain link fence.

"Is it gone?" she asked when he came back in.

"Yes," he said, running his hands under the faucet. "I took care of it."

Holly paused with a salad bowl in her hand, but she didn't ask any questions. She didn't want to make him lie.

Holly and Sean met in college when they lived across from each other in Shepard Hall. Holly was a performance studies major; Sean was doubling in economics and English. He'd seemed very well balanced. Numbers and words. Now he had a job in numbers that allowed him to work from home, where he spent half his hours struggling with words. There was a screenplay inside of him. He was coaxing it out with whiskey and a typewriter. There was no rushing the process.

Holly waited tables at the Heartland Café. Between shifts, she went to auditions and memorized scripts and acted out small parts in local Chicago theaters. She had played an agoraphobic painter, a Victorian maid, a snail with social anxiety. These were her specs: Caucasian, 5'10", brunette, slim build, tattoo of a hummingbird above her right hipbone. The back of her headshot listed the following skills: tap dance, juggling, bird impressions, good with animals and children.

After her roommate moved out, Holly counted up the years she and Sean had spent dating. Sure, there were a few breakups mixed in, but all in all, it added up to nearly five years. That seemed long enough. Sean did the numbers thing. If they moved in together, they could probably save over three hundred fifty dollars a month each. It was a decision that made itself—a no-brainer.

They chose Andersonville. They could afford it, and it was a move in the right direction. Everyone moved north to south, neighborhood by neighborhood until they reached the Gold Coast. They either stopped there or they had a baby and returned all the way north to the suburbs.

In Andersonville, they were near three independent theaters, as well as the Swedish Bakery, the Hopleaf, and the little Taste of Lebanon corner store that served the best lentil soup, for only a few dollars a cup.

They found a place within six blocks of Lake Michigan, the second floor of a duplex. It was bigger than what they envisioned but surprisingly cheap. An extra two hundred thirty dollars in savings each month.

"Best deal in town," the landlord had said. "Can't find another place like it. Hardwood floors everywhere. Look at these windows. Look at these countertops. Imagine slicing tomatoes on these babies."

"They're nice." Holly ran her fingers along the black marble. "This place is really nice."

"What's the story?" Sean said. "Why so cheap?"

"Oh, you know." The landlord crossed his hairy arms. He'd kept his sunglasses on indoors, even though it was cloudy out. "These old houses. They have history. The plumbing's old. No complaints from my last tenant though. She wanted to be closer to her parents. It's not like she died here or anything."

He laughed, so they laughed, too.

They searched the address later for grisly news stories. Nothing came up, so they called to submit their application and first month's deposit. The landlord congratulated them on money well spent. "The kitchen itself is worth its weight in gold. You'll like cooking in it so much you won't *want* to eat out. And downstairs is empty right now, so really, you'll be getting the whole house."

"We can use the downstairs, too?" Sean asked.

"Well, no. I'd have to give you the key."

"Can we see it?" Holly said.

"No. I'm still fixing it up."

He was a strange man, but the unit was lovely. High ceilings lifted up over the expansive living room and a large bay window looked out onto the quiet street lush with trees. A narrow hallway led from the living room past the bathroom and bedroom. Off to the side of the kitchen was a small sunroom where Sean could set up an office. The kitchen opened out to the deck, where Holly imagined planting flowers and herbs, growing her own mint and basil.

Now that they had moved their things in, the place felt less inviting, less like they could call it home. They tried rearranging the furniture, a difficult feat while unpacking. They'd push all the boxes out of the way and move the couch along the wall, then set up their small circular dining table next to the bay window. A few days later, they would do it again, moving the couch back to its original place to create the sense of a walkway and trying the table where the couch had been. Finally, they chose Holly's purple armchair for the window view. A place to sit and read and be calm.

They went to the Brown Elephant to find a lamp and a little end table to place beside the armchair. Sean found a painting of a nude woman sitting between two trees as well.

"It's cool, right?" he said. "It looks like a Dalí or one of those paintings where the man's face is an apple."

"You mean Magritte," Holly said, immediately sorry for her supercilious tone.

She'd always found Sean's grasp of art a bit shallow, but she tried hard not to let it show. The painting was one of those illusions where the foreground and the background switched. One moment, you saw a woman seated beneath two trees on a stone block etched with mountain. On second glance, the drooping leaves were actually slanting emerald eyes, and the woman herself a nose. Her hips flared out into nostrils, and the mountains beneath her shaped the lips.

"Do you see it?" Sean asked. "Do you see the face?"

It felt played out to Holly, but she helped him hang it up over the fireplace.

"That's what we need," Sean said. "More art on the walls."

"I think we just need time. And we need to unpack."

It was becoming a situation, their boxes. She could never find anything. Whenever she thought she knew where something was, it would show up somewhere else, or back inside a box. Her things, his things. No end to either.

"We can't keep living like this," she said. "We're adults now."

Adults cohabitated and made budgets and unpacked their boxes and sliced their vegetables on marbled counters. Now that they lived here, they would be adults.

"Let's meal plan," Holly said. What could be more adult than that?

Sean beamed at his painting. "I feel more adult already."

Only then did the leaf eyes really stand out to her, taking

over the foreground. It was no longer a peaceful painting or a reminder to meditate. The eyes were watching.

When Holly woke in the middle of the night, she could have sworn someone had called her name. Sean was asleep. Sean was a very serious sleeper, his face always contorted in concentration. His slumber never looked relaxed. Mildly tortured, maybe. The childlike tuck of his hand underneath his cheek was a strange contradiction.

She tried to find comfort in the warmth of his back and the rhythm of his light snoring, but her pulse was frantic. Not because of a nightmare. She couldn't remember any dreams. The ceiling fan whirred in smooth circles above her, the blades blurring into invisibility like insect wings. Holly grew hot so she kicked off the covers. Sean grunted. She watched the fan spin until morning.

Going to work was a relief. She made the same laps around the counter bar and the lounge. She took the same orders for over-easy eggs, a side of hashbrowns, a Reuben sandwich. She knew where everything belonged.

At work, she prepared for auditions by taking lunch orders as her favorite characters, her dream roles: Jane Eyre, Emily Dickinson, Madame Defarge. Some of the regulars knew her game and played along. Some of them even ran lines with her, just for fun.

When it was time to go home, her chest tightened again. Drops of rain stung her face. She walked hunched against the wind, sharp gusts rising off the lake to drive the summer away. It was not that she didn't enjoy living with Sean. It was the house she didn't like. There was something wrong about it. The whole atmosphere changed in density when she entered, the mustiness growing thicker as she trudged up the stairs. The door to their unit was not entirely closed. When she stepped inside, someone else was there. A woman with a shock of white-blond hair sat in the purple armchair, looking intently out the window.

"I'm sorry," Holly said, flinching with embarrassment as if she had walked into the wrong house, or maybe the wrong decade.

There was something unearthly about the woman, her loose white dress from another era, her thick platinum hair wound in a long braid. The knit shawl slipped from her shoulders as she turned toward Holly.

"Oh." She sounded surprised, turning her head with curiosity. "Hello."

Holly almost turned to go back down the stairs. If she retraced her steps, maybe she would find another staircase into the right era. But then came Sean, ambling down the hall with two tumblers in his hands.

"You're home," he said. "I'll fix you a drink."

The woman rose to accept her drink before Sean went back down the hall.

"I'm Juliet. You must be Holly. I've heard so much about you."

Holly tried to recall who she could be. Did Sean have a cousin in town? Was she a coworker? "Have we met?"

"I'm your new neighbor." She moved closer as if to hug her. Holly crossed her arms to fend it off.

"My fiancée and I just moved in downstairs. Geoffrey went to work today and I had to supervise the movers. They moved the furniture but left all the boxes on the street. Thank God Sean was here. He's so nice."

Sean came back with another tumbler. "Did you know Juliet here works in film?"

How would Holly have known that? "I didn't know there was much film in this town."

"It's mostly advertising," Juliet said. "But sometimes I get freelance work as a script doctor. I studied dramaturgy."

"Dramaturgy," Sean said. "Isn't that terrific?"

His smile looked so stupid.

He was already a little drunk. Holly could tell. He pulled over a chair from the dining table and sat straddling the seatback. They'd been talking about movies and he wanted to continue. Holly mentioned her abiding adoration of The Craft, but Sean already knew this and Juliet didn't seem to care. Her participation was unneeded. She allowed her eyes to grow heavy and the whiskey to overwhelm her sleep-groggy head until Juliet exclaimed, "We would love to join you for dinner. Thank you so much."

Holly fixed her eyes on Sean, but he was looking at Juliet.

"Let me call Geoffrey and tell him to come upstairs when he gets home," she said.

After Juliet stepped aside with her phone, Sean shrugged. "We're being good neighbors," he whispered. "Don't worry. I'll help cook."

It was chicken cacciatore night, shrink-wrapped thighs already thawed in the fridge. Sean grabbed an onion to begin slicing, but then Juliet joined them in the kitchen, and it was on and on about the Blair Witch Project again. Utter accidental brilliance, Juliet quipped. An artistic coup, crowed Sean.

Holly rolled her eyes so hard it made the onion sting twice as bad.

"So what's stopping us from making a film like that?" Sean said.

Juliet tilted her head thoughtfully, dramatically. "Crippling self-doubt?"

"You have cameras. Holly is an actor. I have three-quarters of a script. We could definitely make a movie."

Holly handed him the bundle of butter lettuce she had slotted for Thursday. "Let's make a salad first."

Sean palmed the lettuce like a football.

"There are definitely horror elements in this screenplay," he said. "I really want to explore that more."

"Maybe you should watch *The Craft* with me," Holly said. He'd never wanted to before. Last she checked, he'd been writing about quirky families with large fortunes and strained relationships. The time before that, it was sad loners and the weird women who changed them forever. Three-quarters of a script seemed like a lot. But the last script was also about three-quarters complete before he abandoned it entirely.

"I'd love to read it," Juliet said.

"So where did you study dramaturgy?" Holly asked, just to claim a place in the conversation.

Before Juliet could answer, a knock sounded at the door.

"That must be Geoffrey."

Holly left the two in the kitchen and walked back down the hall to open the door. "Welcome—"

Geoffrey blinked at her from behind his thick-framed black glasses. "Holly," he said. "What are you doing here?"

"Geoff." Holly turned and looked back toward the kitchen "Sean, Geoff is here."

During the junior year breakup, Holly spent many hours sitting across from Geoff's owlish, blinking eyes. They had met in Calculus. She was failing, for the second time, and Geoff offered to tutor her. She accepted eagerly, well aware of Geoff's poorly hidden crush. When Sean 180'd back to her, she'd hesitated about leaving Geoff and his gentle, diffident ways, enough so that the brief relationship became a sore point. Other-guy, Sean called him. Sometimes, the replacement, the temp, or just: *that guy?*

"Geoff." Sean rose from his chair. "So you're Geoffrey. Geoffrey with a G." A faint blush crept up his neck.

"This is my fiancé," Juliet announced.

"We're so happy you're here," Holly said.

Geoff blinked. "I brought a lemon roll."

"Wonderful."

Holly brought out the dishes so they could all busy themselves and take a moment to recover. It was not implausible for Geoff to move in below. Many of their classmates were scattered throughout Chicago. Still, what were the chances? She left the others to puzzle this out as she served the chicken.

The table was small so they ate too close together, elbows everywhere. Only Juliet was unfazed by the awkwardness. She was delighted, in fact, that they had all known each other. "Not very well," Sean clarified.

He and Geoff toed tentatively at polite conversation, each figuring out what the other had been up to and who had been more successful. Geoff worked as a data analyst at a large bank downtown. Holly was uncertain if this caused Sean to envy or pity him. Men were like dogs, she thought, sniffing each other's assholes and clamoring around until they determined who was alpha.

"This chicken is delicious," Geoff said.

"I'm glad you like it." Holly smiled at the memory of his soft-spoken compliments, his small kindnesses. His dark, almost black, hair still fell across the side of his face in the same way, over the edge of the thick-framed glasses. During college, he had encouraged her to pursue a fledgling interest in developmental psychology and early childhood education, fervent in his praise of financial stability and Roth IRAs. He had an ingrained practicality, borne from his middle-class or Midwestern background. Sean had none of that and found it exciting for her to be an artist. Another sign that affirmed her decision: A week after Sean asked to get back together, she got the role of Ophelia in the school's production of Hamlet. With the rehearsal schedule, she had to drop Psych 101.

Sean was watching her coldly. She felt it from across the table. The jut of his chin betrayed his hurt feelings. She had revealed too much in her reminiscing. She blushed, even though she wasn't sure what it was, exactly, that he had seen. She tried to think of a surreptitious way to apologize, but Juliet began to talk—did she ever stop?—and Sean turned away.

"Let's make a movie together," he said to Juliet. "I'll adapt this screenplay however you want to dramaturg it."

"Will you?" Juliet clasped her hands and tucked them beneath her chin. "That's just lovely. Could I direct it, too? I really feel that I was meant to direct."

"I'll say," Geoff said.

Holly raised an eyebrow at him. This was where his practicality had led him? He shrugged, looking sheepish.

Sean was still avoiding her even as they began to clear the table. Frustration made her bang the plates as she loaded them into the dishwasher. After all, he was the one who had brought this upon them, inviting strangers over to dinner. It wasn't her fault that strangers turned out to be exes.

Sean left her the dishes to invite Juliet into his sunroom office. They sat behind his desk, faces lit by the screen of Sean's laptop.

Geoff wandered over to Holly, refilling his wine. "To the next Oscar-winning partnership," he said sardonically.

Holly wanted these people out of her home. The quickest way was to serve dessert. Geoff stood back as she attacked the lemon roll.

"How did you meet Juliet?" She worked hard to keep her voice civil.

"Friend introduced us."

"When's the wedding?"

"Soon, probably. Juliet's very eager. Most of her friends are married. We're still figuring out the details."

"Well, congrats. She's very lucky."

"And you're still with Sean, I see."

The way he said it alerted Holly to a new sneaking cruelty within Geoff. Juliet's influence, no doubt. She looked over at Sean, rummaging through his messy filing cabinet now with all his red-lined papers. He hid his hopes with self-deprecating comments and unquestioning deference. Holly's heart swelled for him.

She turned to Geoff and said lightly, "He's the best. We'll probably get married soon, too."

Later that night, she wanted to tell Sean how she had stood up for him, how he was, without question, the better man. But a rift had come between them and though they lay down side by side, there was no touching him or knowing his thoughts. They did not kiss or even wish each other good night.

"How strange for them to move in *here*," Holly said.

"Juliet was nice," Sean replied, after a pause.

"I don't know about that."

"Of course, *you* don't."

"What is that supposed to mean?" She looked over at the back of his head.

"Nothing."

She knew what he meant. This was about Geoff. She could have told him that no feelings remained for her, that Geoff was free to date or marry whoever he so pleased as long as she didn't have to serve this person dinner, but if Sean wanted to be a baby about it, then fine. Whatever.

She fell asleep quickly, exhausted. The animal buried in the corner of the yard crept out of the dirt, still headless, a quivering mass plagued by flies and larvae. All night, the animal-beast trod inside her mind. When she woke at morning, she was sluggish and bad-tempered, not at all refreshed.

What did Holly love about Sean? For starters, many things. The way his sandy hair got increasingly mussed as he ran his hands through it when he was writing. The way he was just a tiny bit shorter than she was, even though he wouldn't admit it, but she knew it was true because of the way she could rest her head on his shoulder when they hugged.

Once, during the middle of a fight, in the early stages of getting back together when you were never sure how much you really mattered or how quickly it could fall apart, he said, "Even though you make me want to put my head through a wall, I still *care* about you." It was the sweetest thing a man had ever said to her, far more convincing than Geoff's timorous declarations of love.

Geoff would have been steadfast, she thought, had she given him the chance. No point in dwelling though. He could make his declarations to Juliet instead, whenever he was able to see her. So often, Holly returned home to find Juliet reading in her armchair or laughing in Sean's office.

Even when Juliet was not there, traces of her lingered. Her scent was like overripe fruit. Sweet, sickly. Once, when Holly ran the shower, the water rose up to her ankles. She looked down to inspect the drain and saw swirls of blonde, nearly iridescent hair, strands of it clinging to her ankles.

"Their shower broke," Sean explained.

"It's so rude. She could have at least cleaned up."

Holly went down the back steps to take out their garbage—among it: Juliet's hair, Juliet's napkin with its brush of lipstick, Juliet's used teabag. She stopped outside the downstairs unit. The lights were on but curtains blocked her view. They didn't block the sound: Juliet's moans punctuated by Geoff's deep grunts. Holly didn't want to listen, but the pitch was changing, pleasure veering into a pain. A ragged shout—was that really Geoff? Panicked cries from Juliet. Was somebody growling? Suddenly it seemed like the growling came from beyond, somewhere in that darkest corner of the yard. She dropped the garbage at the bottom of the steps and fled back up the stairs.

The next time she saw Geoff, her cheeks flamed as she tried to forget.

"Juliet here?" he asked, curt.

"They're in the office."

"She asked me to pick up a treat." He held up a box from the Swedish bakery.

It was a big night, apparently. Juliet wanted to celebrate. "We need wine. Or whiskey, or gin, or something."

Sean emerged from the office behind her, disgruntled. Holly could tell how hard he had been working by the tufts of hair sticking out in every direction.

"Did you land the ending then?"

"Who needs an ending?" Juliet chirped. "We've got our perfect ten. Ten good pages."

"We decided to go a different direction," Sean said.

"Ten pages?" Holly couldn't hide her surprise. For weeks now, Sean had been making notes on a large sheath of paper. A hundred pages, at least.

"Perfect for a tidy short film. We can shoot and produce it on our own, send out screeners, enter some festivals, see where it goes."

"They're good pages." Sean nodded, resolute.

After the drinks were poured, the mood was subdued. They ate their marzipan somberly.

"This would be the perfect place to film," Juliet said, studying the window and the ceiling thoughtfully.

"You want to film here?" Wasn't it enough that they did the writing here?

"You get such good light upstairs. Anyway, we can't do our place. It's haunted."

Geoff groaned. "This again."

"I'm serious," Juliet said. "How do you explain the spoons?"

"What spoons?" Holly asked.

Juliet explained that after she had come home from an advertising gig a few days before, she found all of their spoons lined up in a row along the countertop. Geoffrey had not done it, and she certainly hadn't. Yet there they were, the spoons in a row.

Holly felt a chill. Above the fireplace, the slanting leaf eyes seemed to turn to her, their serrated lashes accusatory. But what had she done? She had touched no spoons.

"We need to talk to the landlord," Geoff said. "Someone must have our key. Do you know who lived here, before us?"

"No one," Holly said. "The unit was empty."

"There were claw marks on the wall, too," Juliet said. "Behind the front door. Three long claw marks."

Holly thought of the animal in the backyard, the long gashes down its body.

"I'm sure that was always there," Geoff said. "We just missed it on the walk-through."

"That landlord," Sean said. "He's shady."

"Do you have marbled countertops, too?" Holly asked.

"Excuse me?" Juliet said.

"Never mind. What's your place like anyway?"

"It looks just like your place," Juliet said, and then she sighed. "But I wish we could stay up here. It feels safer."

Holly shook her head. "If you're haunted, then we're haunted, too."

Once she said it, she knew it was true.

In the script, the woman's apartment is also haunted. The character inherits the place from her grandmother who made a pact with a demon, now back to collect.

"You could play the lead," Sean said after their guests had left, trying to bargain the use of their space.

"I'm not sure it's my thing," And she really didn't want to spend more time with Juliet.

"It's my thing, though. And you know, you could be a part of it."

"I'll think about it, okay?"

Production plans continued without her. Sean hosted a whole slew of Juliet's industry friends — production assistants and lighting specialists and the best sound guy in the city.

"But why is he so messy?" Holly asked. These guests she'd never met littered the place with beer cans and cigarette butts and bits of crinkled paper.

"He's a nice guy. He's just fiddly."

So many mysterious visitors. Only Leaf-eyes saw what they all did, but Leaf-eyes was never going to tell her anything. Holly disliked the painting even more than before.

Whenever she studied scripts and reviewed casting calls in the living room, the eyes would distract her as the painting shifted. When all the disparate objects and the spaces between them connected, the face of sky and desert and leaf would grow large enough to loom out of the painting. The eyes would appear to follow her around the room, sometimes mournful, sometimes condemning.

She felt the eyes even in the kitchen as she stood at the sink watching dishes. Now they were coming from outside of the house, studying her as she became the woman trapped in the painting. She turned off the faucet and looked around. The refrigerator hummed on. She checked the spoons. They lay nestled in their drawer, unremarkable. Holly walked over to the door that led to the deck and pressed her fingers against the glass pane. She could see nothing, with the light in the kitchen illuminating the darkness outside. Anything could be out there. That was the riddle. When you were inside, anything could be outside. She wondered if the woman in the painting felt the same.

"I don't know if the role is right for me," Holly told Sean. "I mean, I've never worked on camera before."

"Juliet will help you out. Lots of actors do both."

She did not want to do both, and she did not want Juliet's help. Juliet was the right person for the role, the perfect image of a haunted lady lead. Pale and petite, eyes as wide as a lamb's.

"It's not like you have any other roles right now." Sean didn't have to point this out.

"I like to keep my schedule open."

"That's the nice thing about film. We only need two weekends to film. All the work is in post-production. You don't even have to memorize anything."

She was unpersuaded.

"Can't you do it just once? For me? It won't kill you. Wouldn't it be nice to do a project together?"

"I mean, yes, but..."

"You don't care about my work. You don't want to be a part of it."

The unfairness of it. What did he think, that Juliet took him seriously? That she would pick him over Geoff, just as Holly had, and move in upstairs? Juliet would never stick around. Two years tops and she was gone. Who would read his scripts then? Who would take care of him? What would happen if he got sick? Not with cold or flu, but something horrible. Something that caused blood in the bowels. And he would be all alone. The thought of it brought tears to Holly's eyes. Poor, withering Sean. Her throat tightened. Couldn't he see how much she loved him?

"I do care," she said. "I care a lot."

"We barely spend time together anymore."

"Because you've been so busy. With this project." By project, she meant Juliet.

"Which you could be a part of, too."

"I guess."

"So you'll do it?"

What else could she say? It was a done deal, signed and sealed with a kiss.

It stormed all morning the first day of their shoot. Holly thought it was atmospheric, but Juliet said it ruined the ambient light. There was a whole crew for lights though, each person dripping rain into the hallway as they arrived with wet coats and umbrellas. They moved furniture around and set up tripods and marked things up with tape, shouting over each other the whole time. Someone brought bagels, but they were already stale.

"Renee can get you started on makeup," Juliet said to Holly. "Remember, the camera's a lot closer than the stage. She'll take care of you, though. Just remember, you need to act with your face."

"I always act with my face," Holly said, but Juliet had already moved on, cornering Sean with her giant clipboard.

The makeup artist set up her station in the bedroom and dusted Holly's face with powder.

"You've got great features," she said. "Very prosaic. Like, your face will always remind people of someone else's face."

The door opened and Geoff peered in. "They told me I could come in here to stay out of everyone's way."

Holly shrugged and waved him toward the corner. She didn't know why he was here at all. He slid to the ground and opened his magazine. He was reading The Economist. Nothing frivolous for Geoffrey. But really, his eyes didn't even move. He simply stared at the pages.

"It's probably quieter down at your place," Holly said. "If you want to read."

"And miss all the fun?"

"Does it bother you? The two of them working together so closely?"

He seemed to consider this. "I happen to trust my partner. Implicitly."

Why did he work so hard at being annoying? And what did *implicitly* even mean in that context?

"Then I wish you every happiness."

"It is what it is." He turned back to his magazine, flipping another page.

He was still nose-down in the pages when they moved back into the living room. It was time for the first take. Suddenly, everyone stopped what they were doing to watch.

Holly was given a series of marks, some to stand on and some to rest her gaze on. She was supposed to walk through her living room as if it were the first time she'd seen it while conducting a one-sided phone call.

"Use your face, Holly," Juliet said.

An echo followed from Sean. "The face."

Take one evolved into the take six, take seven.

"It would be easier," Holly said, "if someone else were in the scene." She scanned the faces of the crew, all professionally blank. There was no one to riff with, no one to push against.

"Pretend you're talking to me," Sean cried, hands outstretched with misplaced dramatic tension. His desperation was not for her. He was begging her to get it right for Juliet.

Geoff spoke up from the row of bystanders along the wall, "Maybe you should consider the psychology of your character."

"Let's try another scene," Juliet said.

They were filming living room scenes in one day and then

kitchen and bedroom scenes the next. The sequence was all out of order. Holly moved from moment to moment as best she could. Wonder, then terror. Acceptance, then a spurt of defiance. Everyone lived and remembered in fragments, she told herself. So what if time rearranged itself? In the end, all the pieces were yours. Didn't matter if you didn't like the story. You just had to find another way to tell it.

"I need to take a break," she said. The lights were making her sweat. "I need some air."

She couldn't step out from the back, because Juliet wanted to meet with Sean in the kitchen. Holly went out the front instead. The hallway smelled like mold from all the dampness. Downstairs, the door to the unit below was slightly ajar. She had not been invited over before. Given how much Juliet hung about upstairs, it was rude that no welcome had ever been extended. Holly deserved entry.

The smell was overpowering. Too floral, too sweet. Like it had been laid on extra thick to hide something rotten underneath. Everything looked normal on the surface. His shoes, her shoes. Coffee table books about art and photography. It could be any-one's home. Weren't their walls supposed to be gouged with claw marks? Didn't demons come to play with their silverware?

Holly bound down the hallway. The kitchen was laid out just like upstairs, but the countertops were not marble. They were butcherblock, the wood grain stained with red. Tomatoes, right? Dirty dishes waited in the sink, a half-empty mug stained with Juliet's red lipstick.

Holly opened a row of drawers, silverware in the last one. A jumble of footsteps above her, a door slamming shut. She grabbed the spoons and laid them out on the butcher block, spacing them out carefully. She wanted to take the knives too and mark up the walls, show them where to keep their line of vision. She wanted to tear up the curtains, rip out her hair, clog the drain. Was something growling? Was the growling inside her head?

Voices drifted down, burying that low rumble. Sean and Juliet were standing outside on the steps above her. Holly slipped out the back door and hid under the stairs.

"Overall, it's going well. Right?" That was Sean, achingly deferential.

"Yeah, we're getting somewhere. We've got a great crew. I just don't think Holly has the right passion, you know?"

"She's a wonderful stage actor."

Appreciation unfurled warmly from her stomach, but then Sean continued. "She was the most dedicated snail."

Juliet snorted. Holly burned.

"She doesn't take me seriously, you know?" Sean said.

"You don't deserve that."

Silence, then Juliet again. "Why can't she take *this* project seriously?"

"Probably because I'm a part of it."

"How can you be with someone who doesn't take you seriously?"

Holly could hear Sean's sigh, the scuff of his foot along the deck. "You're with someone for so long, you know," Sean said. "You don't really see each other anymore. You're more like an impression, a feeling."

Not a very good feeling, Holly thought, her throat tight.

"You deserve better." Juliet's voice was much too soft and intimate.

"It's hard to make a change," Sean said, "after all this time."

"You're young. You don't have to be with someone who doesn't respect you."

How dare he? Hadn't she done all of this—the whole terrible day—for him?

"It's alright," he said. "We're used to each other."

She had done all the things. She had stuck with the good choices, the safe choices. There had not been enough choices. The stage was set before she entered and she'd been given a part to play. Had she looked for other options? Why did it scare her so much, to consider something different, to accept what she wanted?

"Should we go back in then?" Juliet said. "Gotta keep the energy up for the rest of the team."

Nothing could convince her to go back inside, Holly realized. The air was so clean from the rain. She only needed to take a few steps, and then she would be across the yard. She would be at the gate. Simple strides. Not so hard at all.

"Holly," Sean called her name from above. "Where are you going?"

She gave the padlock a hard yank. The click of the lock resounded in her own body. She pushed the gate open. The wet asphalt glistened in the alley.

"Wait," Sean cried.

Too late for him. She was over the threshold and she was not looking back. She glanced both ways and picked a path. Then she picked up her pace as well, trotting, running. The wind picked up the ends of her hair and she was sailing away, racing toward this other person that she knew she could be.

HOME

The night before she was to return to China, Mrs. Liu woke from a terrible dream and knew with certainty that the ghost was sitting upon her chest. Her skin was damp from his condensation and it took several seconds to catch her breath. Hours passed before she returned to a troubled sleep.

In the daylight she was herself again—reasonable, practical, rational. Someone who balanced her checkbook every month and attended church every Sunday. Ask any of her friends and they would agree: she was a most logical and morally upstanding woman, one of the last people who deserved to be haunted by a ghost she did not believe in.

The ghost had come from Grand Auntie Du, a line item in her will when the dear woman passed away twelve years ago. The ghost being a ghost, and Mrs. Liu not a believer except in the Holy Ghost, the inheritance had been easily ignored, until recently.

In the last year, the ghost had gone from an afterthought, or a never-thought, to a daily nuisance, an incorrigible bother. She couldn't count the number of times he had switched the sugar with the salt or stolen her keys only to slip them back into her pocket hours later.

How did she know it was a he-ghost and not a she-ghost? She didn't, but only a male ghost would hide her passport, break the zipper on her suitcase, and transform the jars of codfish oil she had purchased as gifts into capsules of worthless Vitamin E.

"Where's your passport?" her husband now asked every day

to test her.

He peppered her with advice and admonishment on the way to the airport. Never leave her passport in a hotel drawer. Always stow it in a pocket that zipped, not one that opened invitingly to thieves. Don't just leave it out next to a full glass of orange juice.

"Do you think I'm a child?"

"Pickpockets love to ride the Beijing subway," he said, as if he knew anything about Beijing. "Thieves are faster in China, you know. Just like the flies. Try killing a fly in China. They're too fast. They've adapted. The environment is harsh there. You have to watch your things."

"You just keep our house from burning down, old man."

"And you keep our daughter from wrecking her future. No more of this nonsense. It's time for grad school. Law school."

Mrs. Liu couldn't help the sense of relief as she rolled her suitcase away from him. She wondered if Michelle had felt this elation as well, crossing an ocean to escape her parents and who knew what else. It's just one year, she had said, when she told them she was quitting her job at the nice Internet company to join a Christian music ministry. Now the year was up, and they weren't about to let her stay another. Operation: Retrieve a Daughter. A woman on a mission, Mrs. Liu. A woman traveling alone. Or rather, a woman and her ghost.

She found her assigned spot and clasped the seatbelt shut with pride. Mr. Liu didn't think she could handle this trip. He had lost all faith in her, but it was this ghost wearing out his patience. She couldn't say that, but she had stood her ground. Why should he get to go to China, using up his vacation days when she already had all this time in front of her to fold and unfold.

Around the time Michelle first left for China, the dental office where Mrs. Liu did the accounting replaced her with a computer. Her schedule a blank slate, she would sit in the quiet living room for hours. That was when the ghost crept out from whatever cobwebbed corner he'd gotten lost in. He would tease the curtains and cast shadows onto the wall. Occasionally, his breath would fall over her and pool like a cold lake inside her stomach. She learned to listen for him, allowing herself to hear the creaks in the floorboards, the hum of the refrigerator, the ticking of the clock, until her senses grew sharp enough that she could hear his sighs as well.

Now as he settled in next to her, his presence was like a friend.

Hui jia le, she said. They were going home.

Since the ghost had belonged to Auntie Du, Mrs. Liu could only assume he was from China, too. In which case, they had both been away from home for a long time.

What did the word mean anyway? Neither she nor Mr. Liu considered China home, but like their friends, they still called it jia. This was the same word for family. Her cousins back in China could not even be considered friends, yet she'd dutifully bought them gifts of dietary supplements and designer purses. Michelle said she wanted to learn about her roots, but she was born an American girl.

Mrs. Liu had taken her daughter to China only once, to keep vigil for her father's funeral. The little girl couldn't figure out when it was required to cry or what made it okay to play card games again. Confusion colored her face an indignant red. Anyone could see that the girl, though a miniature of everyone else in the oversized white mourning gowns, had no place there.

Did she herself still have a place? For months, she had been dreaming of China. Each night she walked the rows of empty desks, past abandoned school books opened to dog-eared pages. She peered out dusty windows at the stone fountain to see the lilies blooming in tepid water. The petals shriveled before they could fully open. Laughter echoed down the long hallways, but anger resounded back. She followed the beckoning trill of her best friend Wen to the gate and the red metal doors blocking off the schoolyard. Outside, a dust storm of voices swirled, growing louder, getting ready to descend. Come, they said. Join us. She heard the shy whisper of that gifted young poet, *Take my hand*, and she lifted her own, surprised by her aged skin, dry like the lilies, reaching forward to push open the door. She was almost there, she was almost ready, more so than she had ever been, and they were almost out of time so she must hurry, *Wait! Not without me*, but the plane hurtled forward, lifting her away as it nosed up against gravity.

Ghost was delighted.

Grand Auntie Du had raved to him about heaven, which was a place he would never get to go, she'd added. His plasma was besmirched by a stain of sin that could only be washed clean by the blood of Jesus, and through no fault of his own, Ghost had not been baptized. It was simply his fate. She would make sure he was cared for.

Yet here he was, wisps of clouds floating by as the plane surged ahead into angel lands. Maybe if he pressed himself tight enough against the oval window, Grand Auntie Du would catch a glimpse of him. My word, she would say, you haven't aged a day.

He waited and waited, but there was nothing but cloud. The geometric patches of land and the gaping black ocean faded away. Whiteness obfuscated everything. Ghost sank back from the window and tucked himself against Mrs. Liu.

At times, a muskiness would collect at his weightless center. This was the closest he ever got to substance. He felt it most when Mrs. Liu was nearby. When he touched her hand, the heat of her skin would radiate into him, as if he too were buzzing with life. As if he, too, had a form that mattered.

Grand Auntie Du had called Mrs. Liu her most fastidious caregiver, but when Ghost was transferred under her care, she all but ignored him. He wept alone until one day, Mrs. Liu began weeping, too. Her sadness seeped out to fill him. First, he was shadow. Then he was breath. He remembered both the years he existed in Grand Auntie Du's basement and the years during which he did not exist at all. He stayed close to Mrs. Liu, hungry for her sorrow, each clear jagged piece of it bringing him closer to something that could be held.

The rhythm of her sad heart knocked against him as a flash of sunlight streamed into the plane. He could sense its heat but felt no warmth himself. Mrs. Liu pulled down the screen, shuttering them back inside a comforting darkness.

Ghost circled underneath her shoulder and around her back, wrapping every tendril of himself against her and squeezing as hard as he could. Sometimes, he could imagine her shattering.

It was hard to breathe in China, the July heat dense with pollution, people, and ash. The Spirit Festival was approaching, and on every street corner, someone crouched over a small open flame, carefully tending to ritual.

Michelle asked, so Mrs. Liu quickly summarized the tradition of caring for your ancestors to make sure they weren't hungry, sad, or broke in the underworld. Then Michelle asked more questions. Mrs. Liu assured her that these folk practices were not worth the time. It was one thing the government was right to stamp out. What's more? Paganism was bad for the environment, all the extra particulates crowding the air.

"I'm sure there are worse things," Michelle said.

"Well, it makes my eyes water."

She didn't want her daughter to see how the competing presence of two worlds tugged her heart askew. China present was a behemoth, automobiles and motorbikes racing past them to continue through the maze walled with skyscrapers. Every now and then, China past broke through the veneer. She would recognize a face or a particular frown. The name would almost arrive at the tip of her tongue before she realized that the person she was thinking of could not possibly be so young. A smell in the air, underneath the fumes of industrialization, would drift by and snag against a memory. It made her pine for what was no longer there, though she couldn't quite pinpoint exactly what was missing, either. Everything was different, even her daughter.

Michelle had cut her hair short. Not just shoulder-length, but trimmed up to her ears, exposing her pale neck and its lean fragile grace. Last year this haircut would have turned her into a child, but this year it made her look more adult. It was in the way she moved, stepping confidently into the road; in the way she spoke, no apologies or excuses.

"Actually, I've left the ministry. I no longer want anything to do with it."

They were at a café called Alba, near the Drum Tower in that quiet pocket of the city where buildings were still manageable, no taller than the Forbidden Palace. The past was somewhat more recognizable here, either hidden in the alleyways behind the boutique storefronts or preserved as entertainment for western visitors. She didn't need Michelle to tell her that this place where imperial families once lived was now a hub for foreign expats. The menu they perused included gnocchi, pasta primavera, and affogato. She didn't even know what affogato was. A separate menu listed several pages of cocktails and spirits.

"The U.S. has spaghetti and unbaptized souls, too," Mrs. Liu said. "You could find other ministry there."

"I'm not feeling very inspired to minister, is what I'm trying to say. Overall, ministry doesn't seem to help things very much."

The organization she'd joined was primarily focused on a Bible study for young mothers. The mothers were primarily interested in exposing their children to native English. All the best phonemes the church could provide. One of the mothers, however, would roll up her sleeves to show them the bruises and ask what could be done. In America, are men like this, too? Yes, they would say, and then offer another prayer.

So Michelle looked around and found people who could offer more.

"It's a big problem here, you know. No one talks about it, but this group of women—college students—put on wedding dresses splattered with blood and walked through the streets once."

"Really? Why? What an ugly scene. I mean, what if a child saw?"

Michelle had that incredulous look. She pulled it out anytime she had to explain something she didn't think needed explanation, which happened often, when your parents were finding their way through America. It shouldn't happen in China, too, in this place meant to be home.

"What do you mean, why? Because people should know. People should see the ugliness. There's no law here or anything to protect women from domestic violence."

"So you want to study law then?"

"No. I want to help. I am helping. A lot more than I was before, sitting through another self-congratulatory servants of Christ rally."

"What about those letters?" Mrs. Liu could swear another postcard had arrived a few weeks ago. The front featured Michelle kneeling in a field of purple flowers, and on the back was a thank-you note, a few prayer requests, and a plea for funds. Several of Mrs. Liu's friends had signed up for that mailing list. "I posted one on the bulletin at church so people would send money."

"I made a Paypal account so I can still get the money," Michelle said. "Don't worry. I'm putting it to good use. Better use."

Her new job wasn't the most lucrative, but it had greater impact, or at least the potential for greater impact. She was assisting a gender studies student, a Chinese woman working on her PhD at an American university. They were interviewing women in the process of divorce, partnering with a non-profit that provided temporary housing, childcare, and legal support. Sometimes, one of the women would live temporarily at her apartment. Her Chinese was much improved.

"Free room and board," she said. "Sometimes free condoms. That's worth more than a prayer, isn't it?"

Mrs. Liu bristled at such blunt words, but she pushed ahead. "What about you? Do you have a boyfriend?"

Michelle rolled her eyes. What was she hiding behind that? As a teenager, she had lied by acting offended. As a child, she never lied. But Michelle was grown up now, and Mrs. Liu had missed it. Somewhere along this past year, she'd lost a daughter and gained a ghost. How Michelle lied as an adult was a mystery. Through postcards, she supposed, and money orders.

"So, you see," the young woman across from her fanned out her hands as if making an offering. Mrs. Liu pulled her attention back and tried to catch the words dissipating around them. "I'm finding purpose, finally. I'm making my own way in world."

"By lying and cheating people of their earnings?"

"For a good cause," Michelle said. "Hedge fund managers lie and cheat, too, you know. So do tech executives. But these people gave me the money to do something good in the world, and so here I am, a steward of their good intentions."

She was too relaxed to be saying this for the first time. Perhaps there was even a coach, lurking in the background. She could have fallen in with any kind of people. Con artists and frauds. Counterfeit bills traveled all over China.

"Mom. It's fine. Don't worry about it. No one's missing the money. They have so much. Don't tell Dad."

"What's he going to do?" Mrs. Liu tamped down the wave of indignation at the suggestion that her husband would be the more outraged or effective disciplinarian. Was Michelle's unsolicited confession then a sign of disrespect to her own moral example?

Wounded, she took longer than necessary in the public bathroom, which had just been cleaned and was not entirely unpleasant. The smell of Beijing sewers carried a strange, slightly rancid nostalgia.

As she scrubbed her hands with the graying communal soap, a shadow moved behind her. She saw it in the mirror. She turned sharply, but it was already gone. The dim lights flickered as she scanned the two rows of stalls. Behind which door hid what? She waited for one to creak open, pushed by an invisible hand.

Then she steadied herself. "You are being silly," she said.

But even after she joined Michelle in the street, she couldn't shake the sense that she was being followed. She had to resist the temptation to look behind her.

Ghost watched as alarm etched itself into the lines of Mrs. Liu's face. He stood as still as she did, afraid to disturb her focus. Had she felt it, too? The gears shifting. The earth scraping against something else, its shadow or its underside.

Since Ghost disembarked the plane, a faint vibration had hummed through his nebula. An excitement was mounting, filling the air, and now, at the click of a lock, it stilled.

The lull lasted only a moment. A flurry of voices rushed up from the depths below, filling the silence like the rustling of a thousand braced wings.

It was the fourteenth day of the seventh lunar month, the eve of the Spirit Festival. The gates to the nether realms had opened, and the dead were charging out.

The crowd was almost unbearable. Houhai, this tranquil lake where Sun Zhongshan's widow had lived out her old age was no longer a place of repose. The winding path was lined with bars competing for customers, each one blasting out the music from inside so every few paces, you could hear another guitarist crooning off-key. Merchants set up stations selling everything from joss paper to T-shirts that lit up like Christmas trees. Locals had joined the bar-hopping tourists as well this night to send off paper lanterns and little boats carrying candles. All this to light the path home for their ancestors. Such foolishness.

Mrs. Liu stepped around the vendors as best she could, keeping Michelle's red shirt within her line of vision. Michelle had wanted to show her the night markets, but she was no longer used to such large crowds, and she had never liked loud music. Her nerves were fraying.

Ghost followed behind, bewildered as well. Never had he been around so many spirits. All this time, he'd been alone.

Mrs. Liu called out to her daughter. "Isn't there somewhere quieter we can go?"

Ghost watched Michelle's red shirt bob along into the distance. All the colors had grown disorienting. Small flames sparked in the sky, their reflections in the darkness of the water. Some of the spirits followed the flames, stretching into streams of mist and smoke. Ghost tried to call them back, to let them know that these were only illusions, but he found that he could not communicate.

He tried to ask one round-eyed matron where she and her cohorts had come from, but she only shook her head. From her thin, elongated neck came one whistling keen that trembled along his perimeters.

He lagged behind Mrs. Liu and her daughter as they turned down a winding road. Even in these quieter alleys, strange ghosts would brush by. Some, like the woman, had long needle-necks above their voluminous bellies. Others bore diaphanous flames dancing in their mouths. A few of them, in passing, released a belch of air so foul it made him quiver.

The hutong side streets were narrower, but Mrs. Liu found them more expansive for her body, like she had room to breathe.

Sometimes, though, a horrible stench would fill the air, so repulsive she could almost feel it slither against her skin.

The college she attended had been nearby, and she used to visit this neighborhood often. She tried to remember where the bookstore she frequented was, and the tea shop with the talking parrot. Away from the noise and the crowd, the past could seep up more peacefully.

A group of poets used to gather not far from the bookstore, behind large sheltering gates that opened into the someone's private courtyard. She remembered the confident cadence of her best friend's voice reading out loud. Wen's writing changed that last year, became more prose than poetry, more politics than aesthetics. It grew increasingly mature and courageous. It was after one of these readings, while the crowd clamored around Wen, that she met the young poet. He had read with such eloquence and steadiness, yet the same lips that had burnished those bold words turned out to be so shy, so timid. The ash was back in her eyes again. She quickly brushed it away.

"This place is one of the last pieces of Beijing's past," Michelle said, turning. "The government tried to redevelop all the old buildings, and now they want to preserve what's left, but it has to be their version of history, of course."

Mrs. Liu was content to let Michelle explain China to her, but she was surprised when her daughter turned, eyes bright, and said, "Mom. I love it here."

She thought of her old friends, all those empty seats in the grad school. "Life is more difficult here."

"I'm actually living a life here," Michelle said. "What could I possibly learn in a classroom that matters more than all the things I'm learning here? I can't go back to reading about philosophy or logic, or God help me, the psychology of market research. I want to do my work here."

Mrs. Liu remembered sitting behind closed doors with her best friend and that young poet, discussing the world with an urgency that only twenty-somethings could muster. Outside, bells were ringing and ringing; hordes of students on bicycles, riding past.

"I needed to get out, Mom. I needed to leave."

She thought of mentioning those students to Michelle, of letting her know that she, too, had lived moments of passion. But, of course, Michelle did not ask. She had her own story to tell.

"I've never really thought about what I was doing, you know? I just did what was expected of me. I didn't think about what it meant or what I wanted."

"We always tried to do what was best for you."

"I know, Mom. It's just that I need to decide what's best for myself."

"Beijing is best for you? What about your education?"

Michelle's pace slowed. "I met a man here. No, not like that. He was a student protester, only 19 when they locked him up. Five years in prison. He says he still dreams about it."

"Those days are over."

"Not for him. He can't work or travel. He can't engage politically. But he walks. He's walked all over China, talking to people and playing the flute."

"Is that what you want? A romanticized life?"

"Mom, please. Don't you see how fucked up that is?"

The heaviness in her chest sank deeper. With effort, she sighed. "Watch your language."

"They took away his life and still haven't given back a full identity."

Mrs. Liu thought of the photograph she had carried of herself and Wen, the last time she visited in '96. Between mourning her father, she knocked on doors and talked to school secretaries, tracking down names and addresses. She took the train three hours to a small village in Shandong, weaving stories for Michelle the whole trip to keep her from complaining about the heat, the noise, her hunger. They arrived at an abandoned house in ruins. The weeds and wild grass along the front path and the courtyard rose up to Michelle's knees. Her daughter scanned the overturned table, the toppled stools, a cleaver with a rusted blade lying in the grass next to other scattered litter. "Did someone have a fight here?" she asked, wide-eyed. Mrs. Liu knew then to stop searching.

They were coming out to a main street now, cars lined up behind a stoplight. Ghost watched as spirits clawed at a bowl of fruit left outside a convenience store. The peaches disintegrated in the fumes of their malodorous mouths. Not even a grape could fit down the piped necks cinching the billowing bellies. This drove the spirits into mad frenzies. All they hungered for was food. Still, Ghost was jealous of them, following the trails of light to find offerings set up by harried descendants. All he had were these two women, neither of them paying him mind.

He'd thought at first that these spirits would direct him home; that among them, he would find a familiar face, like Grand Auntie Du's, and learn what to do. He wondered if he would spot his own face, or if he even had one.

Michelle raised a hand to hail a cab.

"It happened to so many people," she said. "Did you know there's a woman who's still trying to gather all the names? She waits for family members to come forward. It's the only way to know how many people died."

"No. I didn't know that."

Mrs. Liu climbed into the cab without asking where they were going. Her own name might have made the list, if she hadn't left it all behind. Her last night in Beijing, the bells chimed until morning, an endless stream of bicycles weaving past her window and continuing into her dreams. Students, nurses, doctors. The whole country concerned for those who had fallen sick, too weak to stand.

They were headed back to that place now. She could tell from some internal compass. She must have said something out loud, because Michelle responded, "Sure. We can stop, but we won't be able to go into the square or anything."

As the driver continued forward, Mrs. Liu's trepidation grew.

Ghost pulled in close to her again, the quickening of her pulse distracting him from his own restlessness. She was scared and he could feel it. Her dreams were rising up, even though she was not asleep. Maybe he would be a part of them.

She pictured their bodies mangled and broken, arranged on top of each other. That young poet who had once kissed her so softly it was barely a kiss at all, extinguished. His hold on her life would always be that tenuous, an exhalation left on a window glass. And then there was Wen's face, flashing across the glass in the place of her own reflection.

Clinging to Mrs. Liu, Ghost watched the spectral masses doubled in the windshield, refracting within the raindrops that had begun to fall. They were fragmented like light, as insubstantial as shadow, and yet they were burgeoning. Their electricity sparked within him. He stretched out toward them, catching the edges of their energy. He was grateful when the car pulled over and the women stepped outside.

Something like kin undulated in the distance. It churned with disappointment and called to him with its aimless craving. Too nervous to let go of Mrs. Liu, he drew them over to him instead. An amoebic section broke from the throng and swarmed near, at least a hundred apparitions. He touched each one, caressing their lost contours, searching for the source of recognition.

Mrs. Liu stood on one side of the wide street and felt her entire being stretch toward the other side, where Mao's smiling countenance presided over the empty square and the six arching bridges. There was no way to walk across, to find her way back to those varying intersections where she had chosen one life instead of another.

"Mom? Are you okay?" Her daughter's pride and antagonism were gone, replaced by cautious concern. "Should we go? It's raining."

Mrs. Liu looked up at the moonlit sky and felt the drops of wetness in her hair. "It's just a little rain," she said.

"Dad called before you got here. He's worried about you."

Michelle spoke haltingly, arranging her face and plotting her next phrase. Mrs. Liu recognized her own strategies.

"He says your moods have been off. And you're more forgetful. He wanted me to keep an eye on you and see if I noticed anything. I don't know. Is there anything you want to talk about?"

Mrs. Liu bit down on the inside of her lip.

Around her, the phantom throng thrashed and raged.

Her husband had gone too far. He should have spoken to her first. He was trying to use her, pitting her as leverage against their daughter. She worked hard to keep her voice calm.

"I'm fine. Your father likes to exaggerate."

Michelle was still solemn-eyed. "I'll go back, you know, if you ever need me. But I'm just not ready to leave yet."

Mrs. Liu wondered what she was searching for, what her work entailed, and what risks she was willing to take. "When will you be ready?"

"It's not just that."

She waited for her to continue, but her daughter stayed quiet. Mrs. Liu saw how her stance tensed, but she could not guess anymore at what it was that needed to stay hidden. Michelle had traveled past her reach.

Ghost let the countless wraiths engulf him. Images flashed before Mrs. Liu. Bloodied faces and fallen bodies. He heard the shriek of their exertions, their ardor. She smelled smoke and tasted the metal shimmer that trailed it. Their singed flesh left the back of her throat bitter. Ghost had loitered in her dreams and sifted through her memories but he had never seen these images before. They were consciousness inchoate, the unspeakable and unknowable.

"It wasn't my choice to leave," Mrs. Liu told the phantoms circling around her. How easily they had been erased, forgotten. "Tell me your names."

There were no names for the ones who haunted here. No one had bothered to delineate their passing. They were unbound from their physical past. They existed to break boundaries, and here in their midst was this body with its seams unravelling. Ghost gathered their collective might and pushed in.

"What did you say?"

"Your names."

"What names?" The young woman grabbed her shoulder and pulled her out of the sinking darkness. Her face was kind, but a harshness tugged at the corners of her mouth. Her eyes shined with fear.

She had seen this face before, somewhere far away. "Wen?" She grabbed the woman's hand. "Is that you?"

The girl seemed taken aback, as if she had just been slapped.

"I went back to look for you."

Unforgiving, Wen wrenched her hand free. She had never been found. She had never grown old.

"I searched for your work. I tried to save it."

"Stop," the girl said. "I don't know what you're talking about."

She narrowed her eyes, trying to see more clearly. "Who are you?"

"Mom?"

"What do you want?"

"Mommy," the girl whined. "It's me. Michelle."

Yes. Yes, it was her daughter, for her own life had continued. She had gotten on a plane.

"I'm sorry," she said, blinking away the apparitions.

"Are you okay?"

"Yes. I'm fine."

"You scared me."

"I got tired. That's all."

Exhaustion weighed on all her limbs. The cold crept into her bones.

Ghost nestled into her heart. Its thudding grew closer and closer until he could no longer distinguish it as anything separate from himself. Unfurling with pleasure, he stretched into this place he could finally call home.

"I'm sorry, okay?" Michelle went on. "I shouldn't be taking the money. I'll give it back some day. I'll get a real job and live close by."

What use was apology? The choices one made were so rarely their own and so easily undone by time and fate. Her daughter should embrace whatever choice she had.

"It's okay. Everything's okay. Let's go back now, before we catch cold in this rain."

She reached for her daughter's hand, letting her lead the way. She needed to go, to close her eyes for a moment.

CAMP WISH-SONG

We were assembled on a small beach along the Clark Fork River—left feet planted in the sun-warmed sand, right feet rising into tree pose under the tutelage of our gentle-voiced yoga instructor—when Dinny looked up, one hand shielding her eyes, the other pointing at the sky, and shouted, "Holy Bejeezus! He's gonna fall!"

We toppled out of balance, wind stirring our branches. The yoga instructor shot a dirty look toward our quadrant.

"Look! Look!" Dinny was still hopping up and down, pointing in the distance. "He's right there."

The rock climber dangled like an ornament from the side of the bluff, still holding on for the moment. Though we were at least a quarter mile upriver, we could see his legs kicking, struggling for a foothold. Our breaths stopped. We were silent as if we knew this was the worst part. After we watched him tumble down, limbs tossed side to side, stone tripping after stone until finally he hit the ground, we shared one breath of relief.

The trees of our forest fell out of balance and began to sway. "Did you *see* that?" "What the heck?"

"That was powerful," Dinny whispered, her eyes rounder than I had ever seen them.

Rachel grabbed my hand and held on. I searched out Cecilia, who sat resting by the water. She caught my eye and nodded once, to say that she was fine.

"Everyone stay calm," our yoga instructor said, a tremble in her voice. Her ponytail whipped back and forth as she looked from side to side like a cornered animal.

A small crowd began to gather downriver. Our yoga instructor first tried to usher us back to camp and then urged us to stay put. She got on her cell phone and asked for instructions.

One of the bird-watching kids pulled out binoculars. We circled around him, demanding to see what he saw. "A guy with a yellow jacket . . . there's a girl, a lot of rope . . . oh, a blue heron."

"Idiot," Dinny said. She confiscated the binoculars.

What happened next should have taken hours, but I remember it in a blur, Dinny reporting the arrival of the police, the paramedics. "Bird-boy's right. There's a girlfriend, I think. Hot mess, that one . . . . They're covering him up now. He's a goner, folks."

She lowered the binoculars and we huddled together, looking toward the riverbank as they carried the stretcher away.

They flew him out using our helipad. Dinny called it the hell pad, because it was only used for the worst emergencies. Final destination: Nowhere we could follow. Later that night, we held a moment of silence in the cafeteria. Not a very long one, because he was not one of ours, and because it was pizza night.

The camp director took the opportunity to review the rules, particularly the ones about staying in-bounds and reaching out for help when you needed it. ("A helping hand is just a holler away," Dinny said.) After the speech, those of us who had watched from the riverbank taunted the others, describing his hands grasping at air, describing the cries we never heard.

That night after our cabin mom, Janine, began to snore, Dinny flipped on her flashlight and shined it into each of our faces. "No one's sleeping, right?"

We were arranged on our bunks, me beneath Dinny, Rachel and Cecilia across from us. This was our third summer together at Camp Wish-Song.

"The thing is . . ." Dinny said. "The thing that is most disturbing is the guy didn't even see it coming. He couldn't prepare himself. It just came down out of the sky."

I knew she was talking about death, because the counselors liked to describe death as a giant bird constantly circling above us, swooping from time to time, but we kept it at bay with surgical innovation, targeted drug therapy, and an optimistic attitude. We learned to ignore the bird, because the truth was, it was circling above everyone. Cancer was everywhere. On top of that, there were hunting accidents, forest fires, flesh-eating bacteria, and now, rock climbing.

"Caw caw," I said, to break the silence.

"Watch out, worms," Rachel said. "Maggie's gonna getcha."

"I'm just saying," Dinny said. "There's something powerful about that."

We were quiet as we gave Dinny time to think. Her flashlight shined a circle on the ceiling. I resisted for a moment, then I hooked my thumbs together and flapped my palms to make a shadow bird. Rachel wiggled her index finger like a worm. I dove in. She made a high-pitched death squeal before her finger fell limp.

"Very funny," Dinny said. "How mature."

Dinny was our fearless leader. She flew in from Seattle, an actual city, though really she was from Ethiopia, which was even cooler. She had attended outdoor concerts where the lead singer's saliva christened her forehead, and she knew the garage that once contained Death Cab for Cutie. That year, she wore a training bra. Rachel and I were from similar towns in Montana—her, Bozeman; me, Missoula. Just like our towns, we were interchangeable, light brown hair with light brown eyes, similar heights, matching green Chacos, and identical Glacier National Park hats. Sometimes we fought to distinguish ourselves, but more often we melded comfortably, even holding hands as people called us by the other's name.

"You know what?" Cecilia suddenly said, in her sweet chiming voice.

Cecilia was the youngest. She had just turned eleven. She lived in Sweetgrass, a town of sixty-three Americans huddled next to the Canadian border. She was named after a saint. We loved her most, and she would soon be gone. That spring, she had gone terminal. Either the doctors or the parents had said, *no more*. We didn't know how or why, and we didn't ask. Someone, somewhere, had said, *no more*.

My stomach sank as I tried and failed to apologize for the bird shadows. It was just that I forgot sometimes, and when I remembered, I didn't quite believe it. She was lying three feet away from me, breathing, thinking. Her hand was buried inside the short wisps of her downy blonde hair, and I knew she was fingering the scar behind her right ear, which was what she did when she lost track of things.

"He makes me feel like I'm lucky," she said.

The rest of us were quiet. Then Dinny said, "Luck's got nothing to do with it, baby."

"Get rich or get lucky," Rachel said.

"Good night and good luck." I turned to face the wall.

*

Cecilia died in March, at home in Sweetgrass; it rained in Missoula, strange because it was still winter. Low-hanging clouds drifted around the peaks of Mt. Sentinel and Jumbo, and it looked like the sky had moved closer to the earth. Her favorite bandana arrived for me in the mail, no note. It came in a manila envelope with a big label, my name printed above a barcode, so cold and formal. When it was time to pack for camp, I found the bandana in the corner of my sock drawer, the faded pink fabric wrinkled like paper, lined with lace and dotted with white flowers embroidered by her grandmother. I tucked it into the side pocket of my duffel bag. A thought entered my head that I had better iron it out before I returned it to her, and I savored that thought as long as I could.

The drive to Wish-Song was about two hours. Usually, my whole family came, but dad and Joe were visiting campuses, so it was just me and mom. Dangerous, because all she wanted to do now was talk. Every time I stepped into her car, a new lecture or interrogation would leave us both exhausted and disappointed. Yet she kept trying. So I borrowed my brother's old iPod and listened diligently to Black Sabbath, staring out the window until she insisted that we stop for ice cream.

"Cookies and cream?" she asked.

"Maybe butter pecan."

"You're really growing up, huh."

She didn't say it like a compliment. We ate outside at the picnic tables. The clouds above us cast their drifting shadows onto distant hills.

"You don't look excited," she said, "going back to Wish-Song."

I shrugged.

"I know it must be sad. I'm sure Rachel will be happy to see you. And Dinty, too."

"It's Dinny."

"Sorry. Dinny."

She had a different name, too, that she didn't use with us. Only her dad used it anyway, she'd told us.

The thing with camp was that for forty-nine weeks of the year, it was a tucked-away, separate part of your life, a thing your parents and friends couldn't know, and then for three weeks, it was the only place that existed at all.

"You know, I'm kind of glad your time is up. If I'm being honest."

The rule at Wish-Song was that if you stayed in remission for five years, you couldn't physically attend anymore, due to limited space, staffing, funding, et cetera, unless you returned as staff. This would be my last year.

"Maybe next year you can visit Sasha's family on the ranch. Or we could rent a house on Holland Lake. You could invite friends. Or what about swim camp?" She listed off names she remembered from chaperoning field trips and swim meets. "I just think it'd be great for you to focus on a normal, healthy life. You were never really like anyone at that camp, you know. You were lucky."

Though I already knew it, the truth of it stung. Unlike Dinny, Rachel, and Cecilia, I had never laid on a surgical table or watched chemo drip down my veins. I had Gleevec. A pill a day to keep my particular cell mutation at bay.

My registration was quick and easy, a breeze compared to the paperwork the sicker kids and their parents were filling out. One kid watched me with big green eyes looming above a blue facemask. I didn't even know what she was doing here. She'd probably spend all her time in Clinic.

Mom hugged me by the car. "If you get sad," she said, "we're only a phone call away."

Our room this year was in the Osprey Lodge, the closest cabin to the river, reserved for older or matriculating groups. I was first to arrive in our room. The empty beds with the blue wool blankets tucked tight were quiet as church. I set my bag down on the bottom left bunk, my usual. Dinny would be above me, and Rachel across from her. They hadn't assigned anyone to replace Cecilia.

As I waited, I found the bandana and tried to smooth it out against the mattress. I put it away when the footsteps approached.

Dinny and I stared at each other for one long moment.

"You got really tall," I said, finally.

She smiled, her face warm and familiar again. "Taller than you, at least."

She tossed her bag onto the top bunk. "I like your hair long."

I touched it self-consciously. We always came back a little bit different each year, so there was some accounting at first of the changes. Neither of us could look away from Rachel's boobs, when she arrived. They were real boobs, boobs of substance. Nothing like our own.

"Okay, look," she said. "I got braces. Do they make me look weird?"

She stretched her lips open around her teeth, and we laughed, because of course she would be focused on her braces.

The laughter always brought us back together, and being together was like slipping from a dream back into reality. Here, we were our true selves, only now we were missing a piece.

Each year, after the review of rules and procedures, we opened the welcome ceremony with a candle-lighting. Red candles for our dreams and wishes, our hopes for the future. White candles for friends who had left us, but whose spirits and memories burned strong, or until the end of the wick. Candle-lighting had always felt momentous, but I could not summon any whisper of Cecilia. The flames were just flames.

Two new guys came up to us. Brett and Luke, buddies from Spokane.

"Boy, we're glad to see you guys here," Brett said. "We didn't know what we'd get, but we didn't think this camp was for babies."

"Yeah. All I see are babies," Luke echoed. "Hey. You guys hear about Lance Armstrong's balls?"

I caught their eyes, Dinny and Rachel. What were we in for now?

Brett nudged Luke before turning back to us. "So we're thinking about going down to the river later, sneak out before this thing wraps up. You guys want to come, maybe?"

"Another day, maybe," Dinny said, smiling her sweetest.

"They're going to do small group soon, anyway," Rachel said. "You'll get caught."

"What? Too scared?" Brett said.

We faked more smiles and closed them out.

Janine, our former cabin mom, had always been fierce, a one-armed Valkyrie. It was no surprise to us when she got promoted to assistant director, leaving us with our new cabin mom, Shelley. Shelley had never had cancer, of the bone or any kind. She had a degree in counseling from the University of Oregon, a boyfriend named Kyle from Great Falls, and both her arms. She was very nice to us, so it was impossible to respect her. She gave instructions in the form of questions, like, *Could we turn off the lights now? We all need beauty sleep!* Or, *why don't you head to breakfast so you're not late? You don't want them to run out of bacon!* Instead of a cot, she slept on the bottom bunk under Rachel, where Cecilia should have been. When she talked to us about her boyfriend, she would lean in and lower her voice like we were trading secrets. *Kyle sent me the sweetest text.* She told us about how protective he was, checking in on her every night. He even gave her his father's pocketknife so she could fend against bears. ("What about bear spray?" Rachel asked.) Sometimes she tried to give us dating advice, like, *you have to go through a few bad boyfriends before you find someone like Kyle.*

We dreamed up our own versions of Kyle. Short and balding. At least two chins, but sometimes up to five. He wore T-shirts that hung down to his knees and had a heart tattoo of his mother's name on his left calf.

But thanks to Kyle, we found our way around the cracks in the rules. Because he was working in town, Shelley negotiated for two other counselors to cover her for two and a half hours during afternoon activity time. As she gave in to Kyle's sweaty, pawing hands, doing whatever it was they did, we would tell one counselor that we changed our minds on archery and the other that it was too sunny out for collaging indoors. Then we would stay inside our cabin, pretending this made us cool.

Rachel was first to call our bluff. "I'm bored! I'd rather just to go to crafts and make friendship bracelets." At our skepticism: "What? All the girls at my synagogue make friendship bracelets. Some of the guys do, too."

Dinny suggested the private hike. We put on our best camouflaging outfits (gray T-shirts, khaki shorts) and wandered stealth mode through the main campgrounds, ducking beneath the windows of the art room and hiding behind the stack of kayaks. Prison Break: Cancer Ward. Survivor: Remission Island.

When we made it into the cover of the woods, I was the one who directed us to the place where the rock climber had died. We stood on the pebbled bank, employing all notions of physics to determine where he had placed his hands and feet, where his body had met with the durability of rock.

It was here that we first found it safe to say Cecilia's name.

She had given me her bandana. Dinny had her bracelet with the pink and green frogs. Rachel had Flopso, her stuffed bunny. We had all carried these things back with us to camp, like charms or curses.

"Maybe we should bury them here at camp," I said.

"Instead of keeping them?" Dinny asked.

"I don't know. It doesn't feel like it's mine to keep."

"I keep Flopso away from my other stuffies," Rachel said. "My other stuffies sleep in my bed. Flop-so watches from the windowsill."

"Totally normal," Dinny said. "Not creepy at all."

Rachel shrugged.

"What if she didn't mean for us to keep them, but to do something with them," I said. "Like ashes, right? I wouldn't want my ashes in a sock drawer. Ashes are meant to be scattered."

"Maybe her parents did that?" Dinny said.

"It can be creepy sometimes," Rachel said. "The bunny has weird eyes."

I gave up on them and walked over to the bluff. A few footholds opened up a simple scramble, heading out toward a ledge that loomed over the river. I followed the path up, ignoring their cries below.

"We're not coming after you," Dinny shouted over the river noise. "Did you hear me? You're on your own. We're not coming up."

A few minutes later, Rachel: "All right. We're coming."

"I'm fine!" I called back. "I'll be right down."

I'd reached a perch that jutted out over the water, high enough for the world to shift. I didn't mind taking this moment to be alone. A hawk cried out in the distance. The water below swirled darkly, sunlight glinting here and there. It was deep enough. My knees shook, but I jumped.

The shock of the water was my favorite part, its icy density snatching you out of gravity's grip just when you thought your stomach would rise out of your throat. It silenced the rush of your blood with the rush of its own pulse.

When I got back onto shore, Dinny was waiting for me, stripped down to her underwear. I peeled off my wet clothes and draped them next to hers on a fallen branch.

"To death-defying victories," she said after we clambered up the bluff twelve, maybe fifteen, feet.

"To giving the bird the bird."

The third time, Rachel joined as well.

We held hands and faced the water together, but the force of the fall ripped us apart. I stayed below as long as I could, until the rush of the water filled my head with pressure and my ears began to buzz. Until all I could hear was the two-step rhythm of my heart: *alive alive, lucky lucky.*

Rough hands grabbed my elbow and pulled me up.

"Are you trying to drown?" Dinny asked.

I blinked against the sudden brightness, taking deep breaths. It didn't matter how we honored her, I realized after the pounding of my heart subsided. It didn't matter if we buried her things or kept them forever. She had moved on. The current of the water ran slow and sweet around us, heading determinedly one direction. Time would carry all of us forward, but Cecilia would remain the way she was. Cecilia was complete. This was both, it seemed, something to regret and to envy.

We were late signing into dinner. Shelley was waiting for us, and she had enlisted Janine.

Shelley read off the camp rules from a clipboard. She told us we should know better and enumerated the ways we had disrespected our privilege and the camp community itself. "Now," she took a breath after wrapping up the speech. "What do you have to say for yourselves?"

"Oh, no," Janine stepped in. "Don't give them a chance to make excuses. They know they have no excuses."

We ducked our heads to avoid her glare.

"You will now accept the consequences of your actions." Shelley paused, looking over at Janine.

"Dishes," Janine said. "After-dinner clean-up, plus three days of kitchen prep. Since they've found themselves with so much free time in the afternoons, let's have them put the time to use. I'll be watching you three."

"We'll be watching you," Shelley echoed.

"About time somebody did." Janine turned once as she walked, pointing two fingers at her eyes and then back at us.

Since it appeared that Shelley had caused some amount of consternation herself, how bad could we feel, really?

It was international Cook-a-Thon night. We joined a table of campers spreading sticky rice over sheets of seaweed. Onto these square canvases, we assembled strips of tofu, egg, matchstick-ed carrots, and golden radish, like laying out a sunset. At the table next to ours, Brett and Luke glanced up from their messy sushi rolls, whispering conspiratorially.

I ignored them as best I could, flinging egg at Rachel, whose tongue was creeping out the corner of her lips as she tried to keep the rice from spilling over the ends of the roll.

"I give up." She waved the roll in the air, letting it flop side to side.

"Well, that's a limp one." The boys found their opening.

"You girls enjoy the day?" Brett winked creepily. "Get up to any trouble?"

"Wouldn't you like to know?" Dinny said.

"So, Lance Armstrong's balls." Luke jumped right in. "My doctor knows his doctor, and he told me that Lance Armstrong got fitted with these new balls. You know, like, prosthetics. Only, not really, because it was actually some special growth hormone, so they grew out again purple and see-through? And, get this. They glow in the dark."

Dinny raised an eyebrow. "Kinky."

"You think that's what makes him so fast?"

"I really couldn't say. Hey, Maggie. Didn't your doctor give you some fancy glow-hormone?" She turned back to the guys. "That's why Maggie can fly."

Luke's eyes widened. Brett was unimpressed. "Forget them, dude." He pulled at Luke's arm. "They're full of shit."

"That cliff was real high." We heard Luke mutter.

Dinny narrowed her eyes and Brett rolled his. "Are you kidding me? It wasn't that high. Please get over this superpower thing. Let's go."

"Hold up." Dinny stopped them by raising one finger. "Are you saying what I think you're saying?"

"Think about it," Luke said. "We're basically all mutants."

Brett groaned.

Dinny continued. "What I'm saying is: Y'all were spying on us?"

"We weren't trying to," Brett said, pushing Luke aside. "We just happened to look, and you happened to be there. And I don't think the camp directors would like what we saw."

"What else did you see?" I remembered peeling off my wet clothes.

"Wouldn't you like to know."

He turned and stalked away, stopping only once to urge Luke to follow. We would have stayed out of each other's ways then, except after dinner, we had dish duty, and they had cleanup.

"So what did you do?" Rachel asked. "You end up sneaking out anyway?"

Brett leaned his gangly body against his mop. "Just following suit."

A realization sparked inside me. "You mean you followed us. Did you tell on us?"

"What? No."

"How come they were waiting for us?"

"Because you were late. You should have watched the clock." Brett sneered. "You think you're so smart wandering around camp. We saw you two days ago skulking around like a couple of skunks."

"At least we had our adventures," Dinny said. "We didn't get caught as spies."

I still didn't trust them. "Or did you turn yourselves in just so you could get us?"

"I don't care for the third degree," Brett said, "I've got work to do." Then he got real absorbed with some stain on the ground that the rest of us couldn't see.

We cleaned fast when we cleaned angry. We scrubbed and scoured with a vengeance.

Luke, however, could not take a hint. "Tomorrow, you know, maybe we could do this again. Not clean, I mean, but we could all hang out. You could show us your spot."

I threw my hands up and let the mop clatter to the ground. "Someone explain to me why the nut job thinks we're friends."

It was a bit harsh. I could tell when Dinny stepped in and tried to make amends. "So your doctor knows Lance Armstrong, huh?"

She shouldn't have given him the opening.

"Oh, my doctor knows a lot of people."

His doctor knew a whole village of people in Sweden who didn't feel pain. He knew an Indonesian guy with terminal cancer who could now communicate with cats. According to his doctor, cellular mutations didn't always make us sick or weak. Sometimes, they made us superhuman.

Dinny: "Do all snake charmers have terminal cancer then?"

You didn't have a choice in how your mutations unfolded or what made you superhuman. A woman in Iceland started growing moles that could feel sound vibrations, but the waves hurt too much so she had to get all of them removed.

Rachel: "So how's that different from *cancer* cancer?"

The most unfortunate thing was that most governments were too scared to fund this kind of research.

"You gotta give the guy a break," Brett said, a breathy apology at my ear. "His dad's into crop circles. I don't know what's wrong with his doc."

I was not in the mood to give people breaks.

"Do you still believe in Santa or something, too? Are you just one of those types?" I banged the tray of silverware in my hands down onto the counter, letting the silverware clatter. "Listen. You have got to get real. Some people get sick, and that's what they are. Sick."

Luke's mouth hung open as if he meant to protest but couldn't think of how. His dumb face only made me madder. The anger wasn't reasonable, so I didn't try to reason with it.

"It's cancer. Not some back door into the freak show circus. It's not some fucked up lotto you win. You might be special, but you're sick special, and that's not even that special. It's not special at all. Everybody gets sick. Everybody dies. You can't stop it. You can't do anything about it so you just need to shut the hell up and deal."

When I finished, he was somehow right in front of me, his skin so pale I could see the blue veins around his wide-eyed weakness. For a moment, I hated him. As someone whistled behind us, I reached for his shoulders, wanting to shake him. Instead, I shoved him. Hard. I was taller than him and stronger, too. He cried out, stumbled backwards, fell.

"Seriously?" Brett said with disgust as he rushed to his friend's side.

Dinny and Rachel did not come to me. They eyed me warily.

"Are you okay?" Rachel asked.

Before I could answer, Janine rushed back in, eyes blazing with fury.

*

When Janine pulled me out into the pantry, I prepared myself for a good lecturing. Instead, she was nice. This undid me in the end, made me cry. She gave me a hug and also detention.

When Dinny and Rachel asked, I did not try to dissuade them from the image of Janine's fearsomeness, because Janine being kind was worse. I could see in her face how badly she felt for me, and she did not try to tell me it would get any better.

Although they could still go for afternoon activities, Dinny and Rachel opted to stay with me. Shelley allowed it. The rain picked up through the afternoon, drumming against the roof. Cecilia's rabbit—Flopso—stared at me from the windowsill, rivulets of water running down the glass pane behind him.

"So, you guys want to play Uno?" Rachel asked.

I didn't.

"What about B.S.?" Dinny said. "Cuz that's what this is."

"I know some card games," Shelley chimed in. She was stuck inside with us. "I could teach you poker. Five card draw?"

Dinny rolled her eyes big.

"No, thanks." Rachel pulled out her friendship bracelets. "That's like, the worst poker."

For a good half an hour, we all sat and watched her braid her brightly colored floss.

A truck pulled up in the rain, and we realized we would be seeing Kyle in the flesh.

"I will only be gone fifteen minutes," Shelley said. "More like ten, really. Don't even move."

As soon as she left, we huddled around the window.

Kyle was not short or overweight. He had shaggy brown hair that fell over his eyes, and a light beard. He wore a gray T-shirt, jeans, and hiking boots.

"He's cute," Rachel said.

"Maybe it's not really him," Dinny said.

We huddled around the window as he bent his head to kiss Shelley. At first, he kept his hands on the side of her face, but that wasn't close enough or something because then he wrapped both arms around her waist, and there was no more distance between them. When she drew back, he cupped her head once more and kissed her on the nose. That was the moment I learned to long for years later when I met my bad boyfriends.

"Maybe the real Kyle is at home," Rachel said. "Maybe Stink-o Kyle is locked in the closet, and she hires a fake Kyle."

But none of that was funny anymore.

"Are you going to be okay?" Dinny asked. They were going to be late for cafeteria prep soon. Shelley came back in to move them along. I was cabin grounded.

"Yeah, I'm fine."

My mother, with her sixth sense, rang as soon as they left. Shelley, taking pity on me, stepped out to grant me privacy for my one phone call.

"You want to tell me what happened?"

"Nothing, really."

"They said you assaulted someone."

"I barely touched him."

"And the truancy. You wanted to be there. Why play hooky?"

"We wanted to hang out."

She tried to piece together some kind of lecture but gave up partway, sighing loudly. "You have nothing to prove, okay? I'll see you soon. Your brother's going away next year. We just want you to stay safe."

She said the word safe as if it could weave a protective spell around me, but there were so many things in the world she would never be able to stop. She was as helpless as the rest of us. I wondered if she realized then.

The room echoed with emptiness after we hung up. I was alone for the first time in days. Shelley's knapsack sat at the foot of her bed, and I knew she kept Kyle's grandfather's pocket-knife stowed away in the front pocket. I'm not sure whether I knew what I would do or if I were merely curious to examine something of Kyle's, up close and on my own. I unfolded the blade from an unspectacular black sheath, tucking it back in a few times by pushing in on the release notch. Slipping the tip of the blade into my forearm was not so much harder. My skin gave less resistance than I expected. The pain didn't register at first, and then the sting was only mild, so I sliced down toward my wrist.

The blood seeped out in one bright line at first, and then began to streak like the rain on the windows. I grabbed Cecilia's bandana from under the pillow. If I cleaned this up, it would go away, I thought. My pulse began to pound in my ears. *Alive alive alive.* The bandana soaked through with red, so I grabbed the Kleenex instead, one white sheet after the other crumpling into red roses that fell to my feet and then I fell to my knees. That was how Shelley found me when she came back.

At the hospital where I stayed for a month, the psychiatrists talked about survivor's guilt and detachment and projection, but what I remembered most, and what I still missed somedays, when I closed my hand around the hilt of a knife or some other weapon, was the sense of wielding enormous power—not to deliver death, but to say when.

LAST NIGHT WITH THE BROTHERS K

Dmitri. Now there's a man. Picture that chest hair ready to spring out from behind the stiff cravat. Tug on that, why don't you? Dig your fingers into that fur until you feel the muscles tighten underneath. Run your hands down. Feel his belly flinch. Grab that cock. It's just as big as you thought it would be when you watched it swinging inside his breeches as he was walking toward the captain's house. Length *and* girth. Circle it from the base with thumb and index, and stroke up. Feel the bulge in its contours and follow its curve to the left. (A ragged moan.)

The sounds he makes, they come from his gut. Here's a man who loves with his insides, with his stomach. The way he tosses you onto the bed, grabs you by the hair, rips your shirt. Buttons clatter to the ground as you invite him to hurt you. Even the stubble on his face scratches as it razes your breasts. And when he dips his head between your legs and thrusts his prickly chin against that tender swatch of skin, it's "O Mitya! O *Mitya!*"

When he's through, you'll have bruises. He doesn't mean to leave marks, but everyone knows he's clumsy. Hide the contusions with a scarf, a shawl, a sarafan—there's some Russian garb for you—and go give your alms to the church and your charity to the poor like the good, solid girl everyone thinks you are. Run your errands with a secret curl of heat licking up your stomach every time a cringe of pain makes your cunt remember how good it got.

Virility. Dmitri personifies it. He'll throw you down anywhere. Inside the boat, behind the shed, on the kitchen table. Doesn't matter if you're in the coatroom of an opera house or the washroom of a gambling den, Dmitri is ready to rock.

The trouble comes when you squeeze him into jeans and a jacket and say, "Hey. I want you to meet my friends."

He can't pull off that fumbling grace when you take him out in public. His laugh is always too loud and a second too long. That glass of wine he's strangling in his hand might shatter at any moment. Cold shrimp hors d'oeuvres jump out from his hirsute fingers, and cocktail sauce splatters his shirt and your dress. Oblivious, he tells a joke no one even cares to understand. In the silence that follows, he shakes his head and mutters, "God sets us nothing but riddles, eh? Nothing but riddles.... Ammiright?"

When the man finally clues in to the raised eyebrows and ill-concealed sneers, he piles his plate with lamb chops and takes it to the corner to sulk. He's a bit of a child—incessant demands, no self-control. A boy playing dress-up in military clothes.

Once you see the chink in a tough man's armor, there's no going back. Soon, there's a crack across his whole veneer. You begin to lose patience when he storms over, night after night another fit of passion and a touch too much to drink. There he goes knocking down the furniture as he wrestles his big emotions. "Beauty!—Beauty is a—is a—TERRIBLE thing! Awful thing! And man! [Hiccup.] Man is too … [Constipated squint.] … broad. Too, too broad, indeed. I would have him narrower! [Belch.] The devil only knows what to make of it."

Give up any ideas of his burly strength and his hairy resolve.

This is just a man-child weeping for his mother. His whole life's a laceration longing to be healed, and who said you had to be the one to heal him?

He grabs you by the hem. "Let me be accursed!" He pounds his fists on the ground. "Let me be vile and base! Only—only let me kiss the hem of the veil in which my God is shrouded."

You don't need this kind of bullshit. Life's complicated enough. He might be good in the bedroom (and the kitchen, and the billiards room, and the conservatory), but you know from your vast depths of mature emotional experience that sex isn't everything. It's time to get a move on.

And who *doesn't* like Alyosha? Kind, amiable, polite—impeccable manners, sound judgment. Adorable the way he blushes.

Hang up that red-hot bustier and find something more appropriate. A white chemise? A negligee? Dab your wrists and neck with a scent like Angels or Heavenly and make your way to the monastery. You know where your man likes to hang.

The first thing you love of Alyosha's is his hands. What a change from those apelike appendages Dmitri waved around. Alyosha has the hands of a violinist, a piano man. His fingers long and slender, callus-free, not a speck of dirt beneath the nails. The first time they wander close to your breasts, they stop, and he takes a breath to ask permission. These hands don't squeeze or pinch or hurt—they touch you like you're a holy artifact.

With Alyosha, guidance is needed. Be patient; be on top. Soothe away his concern for decency and his apology for male desire. Assure him it's all right, it's perfectly fine, to slide a finger inside and strum a note with that musician's touch. The first time might be awkward, but don't give up; he'll get there. And anyway, not everything is about the sex.

Now, his dick—it's not as big as his brother's, but it's very proper. His balls are the least threatening pair you've ever seen. A little lopsided but tidy, well defined. The right one's bigger than the left. For the first time, you find pleasure in taking a testicle whole into your mouth and sucking tight. Let him squirm a moment before you release. Trace the backside of that arrow-straight shaft with your tongue up, up, up until you feel the ridge at the base of his silk-smooth head. Watch a pearly bead appear at the slit and lick his syrup onto your lips. Keep circling that patch of velvet until you make a pious man shudder, and don't pretend you don't take some pride in that.

Soon enough, he'll flip you on your back and from there, you're off. It's always missionary, of course—remember who you're here with. It takes him forever to come, whether due to religious guilt or his own bashful nature, maybe both.

This is a good man—the perfect man. Your friends and acquaintances love him. "Oh, Alyosha," they cry, "you are just too kind!" They rush to take his jacket, pour him tea, offer him his pick of charcuterie. They hold up babies for him to kiss, air out problems for him to launder, all the while ignoring your new shoes and your attempts to discuss local politics.

In fact, you begin to suspect they all like him better than they like you. Who can blame them? He's so cute and happy and *nice*. Listen to him rhapsodizing about blue skies and sticky leaves in spring. "Ah," he sighs. "Dear friends, don't be afraid of life! How good life is when one does something good and just!" When you're around such a swell guy all the time, how can you help it if you sometimes have the desire to punch him in the face?

Of course, you don't. You can't, not when he's already sorry for what he did or didn't do, sorry for displeasing you, sorry you're not happy. So just get over yourself. The guy is a saint. Look at him, looming above you as you copulate, his face purple from strain and his eyes so blue and kind and so goddamned innocent. Even his priapism is a form of penance. He'd hold a boner for you till the second coming of the Lord.

And you? What are you? You know you don't deserve him. Your friends know you don't deserve him. After every orgasmic high, you sink lower and lower. You fall so low, his gaze—those celestial eyes, clear pools into a pristine soul—can send a shiver down your own besmirched body.

Get out while you still can.

You know it's the right move. You can't live like this, constantly reminded of your own inferiority, put in your place by spurts of self-righteous kindness. Who does he think he is, anyway? He might be the perfect prototype of man, but he's still the son of an old buffoon.

So, yeah. Shake off that gooey residue and take a long walk in the country—a gambol, if you will. Comfort yourself with the knowledge that you are still desirable, you are still quite a catch. You may not be as excellent as he, but at least you can understand what it is to be human.

Find yourself outside the house of that old buffoon. From the garden, you can hear Dmitri fighting with his father. Ignore them. Hang a right to the servants' quarters, trip down the muddy path to the old shack and slip in through the wood-slatted door. There he is—washed in moonlight—Smerdyakov!

The bastard son of the sad beggar maid, Lizaveta's issue. Not a Karamazov by name, but can a rose be any sweeter? Yes, he inherited his mother's stench, which is at first overpowering— think onions and mold. But look into those sensual eyes, brush your fingers against that strong jaw. Despite that sneering weasel face, the unctuous skin and slicked-back ponytail, he still has the Karamazov features. When he starts to kiss you and you breathe him in, the smells combine to make something heady and intoxicating, like wet clay or damp leaves. Take another breath. Isn't this what love is? Becoming attached to someone else's smell?

Strip him of shirt and trou and peruse his pasty, scabby form. His chest hair is coarse and scraggly, his stomach as pale as if the moon left its glow. His man-stump is not worth description, but he does know how to use it. The guy flops like a fish. You've never come so many times. At the end of it, you're the one gasping for breath.

After you've exhausted him, you lie inside that drafty shack that echoes each one of his baritone snores and you feel your sense of self shift back into place. There's no one here to measure up to anymore. No one to compare yourself to and fall short.

Who was it that once said: *Above all, do not be ashamed of yourself, for that is the root of it all?*

No shame in what you're doing here with Smerdyakov, either, but since you're fulfilled, hurry out now. Don't stop to wonder what he's dreaming of, poor man. Don't snag your dress on the door.

You've got back your groove, your confidence, that saucy one-two step. Just in time, too, because you've saved the best for last. Ivan's back in town, and he's dripping with dark and mysterious.

Oh, Ivan. So tall and thin and brusque. Weary from the weight of his own intelligence. You know he's been skulking in the back of your mind this whole time. Ivan's the prize. He's the gem. Ivan's the one you want.

Just listen to the shit he says: "I think if the devil doesn't exist, then man has created him; he has created him in his own image and likeness."

Mind blown. Where does he come up with this material?

Look at him sitting there behind the smoke of his samovar — whatever the hell that is. Another thought strikes, and he waggles a jaunty finger. "It's just one's neighbors, to my mind, that one can't love, though one might love those at a distance."

And yes, that man keeps his distance. You try to have a nice rooftop breakfast in the middle of New York City. Baked eggs and prosciutto-wrapped asparagus. For a moment, his ghostly form shimmers, but then he is sitting across the table again, calmly riffling the sheaves of the morning paper as a few pigeons dust their feathers onto his lap. Then he pulls away and you both sink back into his dacha. You try again, racking your brain for something he'd like — a Shostakovich concert at Carnegie Hall, a staging of The Cherry Orchard — but no. The guy stays next to his samovar, resolutely eating his borscht.

Inside all that heavy smoke and keemun-scented fog, you can barely make out his features, but he sees you. He knows what you're about. You can try to seduce him with your wit and your charm, put on a few costumes and see what gets his gears grinding, but you won't get him. Try all you can to tempt him into the world you're concocting, he's not coming with you.

Ivan gets what the others don't. Despite all that bullshit crap about love and God and the devil, he's right about one thing. If you're to love someone, then you better make sure the person himself stays hidden. Another finger jabbing into air: "As soon as he shows his face — love vanishes."

This is why you leave Dmitri in the alley, howling for his

lacerated heart. This is why Alyosha scares you, all intensity and ardor. This is why you didn't even give old Smerdyakov a chance.

And whoever Ivan is, this is why you don't love him, or the ones who came before him, or the ones who will come after him. This is why you sleep alone at night, trying to conjure up some slippery shade of man who will last you until morning. This is why you love nobody and why nobody loves you.

SWEET SCOUNDREL

She knew before the lines appeared. She knew before she bought the test. Growing up, there was an old woman in the village one over who could tell at a glance if you were, and some of the barren wives who knew they were not would go see her in case her powers could extend beyond sight and inspire them to become so. The barren wives would pay a week's earnings, for what? Useless soups made from fish guts and chicken scraps, her mother had said. Tiantian herself never paid attention. She never cared who wasn't and why not or who was and shouldn't be. Other people cared. Other people talked. She did not. Yet here she was.

Wo you le, was what they said: I have it, I got it, I with it. How did that translate?

Wo you le, she thought. And the lines turned pink.

Robert Cao was unprepared. This had become his natural state. Many years back, he had one foot in front of everyone else. When the sparks of unrest began to scatter across colleges in China, he received his acceptance letter to the University of Pennsylvania. After the ugliness of the massacre in Tiananmen Square, his road to citizenship opened. He landed his first job. His wife joined him overseas. With his connections, her biology degree, and the general idea that the Chinese were diligent, she found work at a lab. They opened 401Ks. They signed their names on mortgage papers. Everything transpired in an upward motion to carry him toward a prosperous future.

And then.

Then came economic disaster, layoffs, hair loss, face loss—everything but weight loss. Returning to China, working for an executive half his age, getting re-educated in how to sing the right praises despite all evidence of incompetence. Then came his wife's scorn, tightly concealed but always detectable. Then came age. Age—and all its embarrassing accoutrements. The minutes wasted in front of the toilet, his life dripping away from him. Tubes shoved up his rectum to inspect the growths along his colon. Nothing to be alarmed about, his doctor said before scheduling another scope, six months later. Then came flabbiness. His shrinking limbs flailing against a growing belly. The exhaustion that swept over him from time to time, utter and complete, like he had been knocked to this shore of life by ten-foot waves, his body so battered and waterlogged he could not imagine lifting an arm, much less standing, walking to high ground before the next wave crashed.

This was what Robert thought as he sat across from his mistress—beautiful, lovely Tian'er. Occasionally, he still felt a jolt, not of desire but surprise, a sudden disconnect in the pattern of his life. Where had she come from? How did she fit into this? At times, he was unprepared for her.

She watched him from the sofa, her body folded into the space between the cushions. The thin plastic strip sat nestled in tissue papers on the coffee table in front of them. She was waiting for him to say something, but exhaustion incapacitated him.

He studied the white walls, stained by the harsh Beijing air. When he invited her to move in, almost two years ago, he told her she could decorate as she wished. After all, she was here yearlong, living in his employer-assigned condo while he toggled between Beijing and Boston. At first, he thought that fear of displeasing him prevented her from adding more of her own furnishings. She always took such care, never offending or inconveniencing him. Later, after they'd more or less settled into the relationship, he attributed it to lack of imagination. Finally, he decided it was lack of effort. Tiantian was one who lived through television and books. She always knew the plot of whatever show was being broadcast and she cried when reading novels. She could live forever in her imaginary worlds, but a child would draw her out, ground her. That was why people had children—to embellish one's life with milestones, to push themselves forward to the next goal and leave their mark on the world. Back home, his daughter's growth and accomplishments were framed in rows of photographs—a piano recital, a tennis match, suddenly her high school graduation. He imagined these walls exhibiting the same rhythm of life in progress, starting again from the beginning, a piece of his old tired self made new again.

"Forget it," Tian'er said. "I'll take care of it. I'll find a nice river and drown myself."

"Why would you say a thing like that?"

"What else is a woman in my position supposed to do?"

Robert blinked as he searched for a response. Though they were in a country of government-enforced birth control, he knew nothing of the actual process for procuring an abortion. There would be paperwork involved. There was paperwork for everything. Documentation—sometimes false, sometimes real—and always, always stamped.

"A child is a gift, isn't it? A mother's greatest joy?" He heard an echo of his wife's voice.

"A mother's joy," Tian'er mocked. "Also a mother's burden."

She pushed on past his silence. "Will you give this child your name? Pay for clothes, toys, school? What if he falls down? Gets hurt?"

Robert moved next to her on the couch. "So. You think it will be a boy?"

Speaking in Chinese, Tiantian had not specified gender, but the image of a child falling evoked for Robert the picture of a boy kicking a soccer ball down a green field. Tiantian herself had been thinking of a bundled-up toddler, sex unapparent, walking through a door and tumbling down a long flight of stairs into nothing.

Noiselessly, she began to weep.

Her long hair spilled forward as she hugged her knees, so Robert could not gauge the distress on her face. He patted her shoulder and rubbed circles along her back, remembering the hours he had spent soothing his daughter after her night terrors.

"There, now," he said. "You'll be okay, we'll be okay, and our son will be just perfect."

Six weeks after Robert's sperm collided with the ovum inside Tiantian's left fallopian tube, the cascading, rippling ring of cells cleaved and coalesced until it exerted a heart to beat. At seven weeks, a face began to emerge, the outline of a nose, a mouth, printed on a mung bean. The buds of arms and legs twitched.

Tiantian felt none of this, on her knees in front of the toilet. Buoyed by Robert's enthusiasm, she could fake an interest in tiny shoes and baby coats, overact her misery to ask for more gifts and money. Before returning to the U.S., Robert left her twenty thousand *kuai* for vitamins and herbal supplements. She set aside half the money to send home to her mother in the countryside and put the rest into a high interest CD.

The day after he left, she returned to work at the KTV. Robert thought she had quit years ago, but she resumed shifts whenever he was not around. She was ten weeks now, and the other women could tell her which clinic to go to, which medicines to take. Later that night though, she began to bleed. She did not notice at first while squatting over the toilet, but when she wiped, blood bloomed red on the tissue. She stared at the bright feathery petals. Sometimes they tested people for insanity by having them read blots of ink. She couldn't decipher what signs her body was sending her, so she cleaned up and asked her friend Bella for a pad.

A subchorionic hematoma tricked her into thinking she had been spared. The baby had changed its mind and would find itself a better mother. Tiantian waited for pain and cramping, but she only felt lightness and relief. She invited two young customers — friendly, foreign, and top-shelf spenders — to join herself and Bella up on the rooftop. They could hear the music from the club nearby and danced to the distant beat. City lights illuminated the tall buildings surrounding them and the world felt wondrously large. She laughed and threw her hands up and reveled in her minor catastrophes.

One of the men draped his jacket over Tiantian's shoulders. He tried to make conversation but his Chinese was rough and his English not much better. She understood *pretty* and *drink* and *sweet*. She was always the sweet one, so she let her eyes drop shyly after they kissed, waved off the vodka and had a beer instead.

They used English names at the KTV, and hers was Sugar, because *tian* meant sweet. Sweet girls were naive. They were flustered by flirting and spoke just barely above a whisper. They never failed to notice when a man's glass was empty or when his self-confidence was low. Sweet girls got pregnant and accepted it as *ming yun*. Sweet girls surrendered completely, even when they were only pretending.

Maybe she knew even then that the pregnancy remained. Surely, she'd realized in the weeks after, but still she did nothing. Let fate run its course. Wasn't that what the *dao* espoused? She let the *dao* do its work as she pored over episodes of the original *Shanghai Bund* on Youku, wondering if her compulsive media consumption would grant her child Chow Yun Fat's soulful eyes or Angie Chiu's sculpted cheekbones, like how mothers before her had tried to create a generation of tyrannical Maos by studying his image.

She went to the doctor's appointment at the clinic Robert had taken her to last time, where she didn't need a residence permit but services were still affordable. She was almost fourteen weeks and the baby was now a creature of some enterprise. She learned that if she shined a flashlight on her belly, the child would turn away and burrow into her womb. It knew a place inside her that she herself had never touched. When prodded the right way, it would curl or extend its premature limbs.

Across the ocean, Robert tracked its progress, too.

"Show me your belly," he would say.

"Don't be silly. Only my boobs have grown bigger."

"Show me those, too."

He called between 7 and 8 p.m. They were separated by exactly twelve hours. She pictured him exactly halfway across the world, preparing for board meetings behind a black desk, fiddling with an arrangement of glass paperweights lit up from the inside with twists of color. When he called, she could pretend he was a typical husband apologizing for working late.

In actuality, Robert called from the parking garage. He propped the phone on the Camry's steering wheel as he ate luke-warm oatmeal packed from home. The wireless was not strong enough to support the video feature on WeChat, but he preferred the photos that she texted later anyway.

He snuck peeks during conference calls and in the bathroom, hidden from his wife. On any day, he could count the number of things Lan said to him: Garbage. Dishes. Driveway. Lan was one of those women whose elegance was epitomized by the word quiet. Even slicing sweet potatoes required the same focused intensity Robert imagined she brought to the lab, presiding over rows of test tubes. Perhaps for Lan, the act of cooking really was as complicated as preparing assays. Her family had come out of fortune, then famine. Until they had no food, they had servants who helped cook it. They did not fare well in the revolution. Robert's family, descendants of a proletarian hero, saved them from dishonor.

Lan did not approve of China. She did not trust economic booms or technological advancements, like the high-speed rail or the subway lines her husband raved about. She did not like that he made his money in China, and she did not like that the promise of an easy life was drawing her daughter there, too.

"People will take advantage of you," she told Tiffany over Thanksgiving dinner. Tiffany had waited until they were all lethargic from overeating to make her announcement. In the spring, she planned to study abroad.

Lan was full of questions about her grades, her credits, and why she would want to leave her friends and that secret boyfriend she never talked about when this was her last semester, but Robert cut her off before she could figure out where to begin.

"Your mother only knows the old China. Beijing is a lively, developed city. I think it's great for you to see the world a bit."

Robert always said whatever it was that would win Tiffany's favor, never bothering to consider consequences. He blithely sailed along, gone over half the year, leaving her to carry all the worry. He knew nothing. She shot him a look to tell him as much, then turned back to Tiffany.

"Shouldn't you stay on campus to work on your thesis?"

"I got my advisor's approval. We'll meet online."

"It's your last semester. You won't miss anyone?"

"We all have to part ways at some point."

She was already collecting her dishes, getting ready to leave. Tiffany was adept at quick exits, always an excuse at hand: study sessions, acapella shows, her roommate's cat needed to receive its anti-anxiety medication on time lest it tore apart their shoes again.

"Let's talk about it more tomorrow," Lan tried.

"It's done, Mom. I booked my tickets and everything."

Silence reverberated after the front door swung shut. Though Robert had only returned a few days ago, they'd already exhausted all the noteworthy updates. Had he known about the study abroad? She didn't want to ask. He offered to help put food away. She turned him down. He was no good at fridge organization, and there was so much turkey left. Like every year, it was too dry. They'd swallowed down what they could.

"Why don't you just go to bed?" She was uncomfortable with

him lurking behind her, his gaze still bleary from jet lag. She'd rather be alone than in a room with someone half-present.

She scrubbed the greasy pans and listened for the sounds of her husband moving through the house. His returns always took getting used to. The stairs creaked as he headed up. The door to the bathroom shut. He could be in there for upwards of half an hour. She tried to grant him the privacy these matters deserved, but she couldn't help waiting for the sound of a flush.

All around her, inside her, patterns were shifting. Her body was writing a new alphabet, etching a unique set of fingerprints onto the clump of cells growing inside her. Tiantian craved the foods she once hated and couldn't stomach the smell of pork. Her nipples darkened. Her belly began to jut out.

Tiantian was unable to hostess in this state, but Kai was a good manager, much better than the ones at the upscale places where she used to work. Kai waived the stage fee and offered her an apron instead. Now Tiantian served drinks and snacks, checked people in at the front desk.

After her last shift, a few days before Robert was due back, Bella led her into an open karaoke room and a chorus of other hostesses shouted, "Happy baby shower!" They brandished balloons and stood around a bucket of *Yanjing* beers.

"Western customs for your western baby." Bella grinned, handing her a plate of frosted sponge cake, layered with fruit.

Tiantian burned with both embarrassment and affection. She didn't even know some of these women, but they were her sisters. She knew enough.

One woman pulled out a birth chart that nobody knew how to read.

"Forget this superstitious garbage," Bella said. "There's no good fortune except what you go out and earn."

"A boy is better insurance," the woman with the birth chart said. "No man forgets the woman who gives him a son."

"Don't let him take the boy to America without you," another woman warned.

"Your luck is so good. An American *laogong*. Do you think your baby will look western?"

Bella scoffed. "He's American but he's Chinese. How can two Chinese people make a baby with blue eyes?"

"Chinese people in the U.S. look different from us," the younger woman insisted. "It's the milk they drink."

"No, it's all the sugar they eat. They grow tall and beefy. They're always hungry for something sweet."

A baby was not a bad thing, they told her. A baby could mean that you were taken care of for the rest of your life. They didn't mention how a baby destroyed your body and ruined your future prospects. She was only twenty-six. So much life ahead of her. If she had stayed in the village, she would likely be married already, weighed down by two little brats. She'd left because she didn't want to be weighed down, yet here she was anyway. No escaping fate.

Nobody wanted to turn a surprise party into a pity party, so Tiantian agreed with them. Robert was a good a man and a good investment. She was lucky, and it was, in fact, true. Robert had stood up for her the night they first met, when his colleagues got too drunk and too rough. He'd continued to support her, never asking questions. She said instead that Robert had seen his fortunes rise, as he was good at managing his money. His wife was ugly and the relationship long dead. He would build them a second home in the U.S.

Kai, who'd snuck in quietly and stayed back by the corner, looked on with a skeptical smirk, arms crossed over her cropped tuxedo jacket. She stopped Tiantian on her way out, waving a red envelope. "Bonus," she said. "Take it. Watch out for yourself, Sugar. If you need anything, you know how to find me."

"I'll be fine. Robert's a trustworthy man."

"Of course. Sure. But you'll learn."

Robert, trustworthy or not, was at least good and decent. He was much gentler than her own father, who died years ago after a fit of rage sent a blood clot into his brain. When she'd told Robert about this, she made it sound as if both parents succumbed to illness.

After Robert returned, he woke early to make lumpy millet porridges and soup that coated her lips with salt. He served them to her with American vitamins and hummed off-key lullabies to her belly at night.

Attentive as Robert was, she knew he lied to her. He swore no more feeling existed between him and his wife, yet he never mentioned any desire to leave her. He said there was nothing he wouldn't give up for the sake of their child. He came home complaining about having to work late, even though she could smell his clothes and his hair, reeking of grilled meats and cooking oils.

When a phone call came late at night and he took it into the kitchen and spoke with soft, appeasing tones, she knew he was speaking to a woman and that this woman was not his wife.

Tiantian cornered him in the kitchen. How could he do this to her? How could he get her into this state and then abandon her? Was he really so heartless, so shameless? Had he been placed on this earth to ruin her? Had she, in turn, been placed on this earth merely to suffer? And if he didn't care about her suffering, then what about the pain of their unborn child?

Her performance left her breathless, dizzy. She needed to sit down. Robert ushered her to the sofa, his mouth working noiselessly. She'd stunned them both. Her hands shook as she tried to quiet this unexpected rage. The baby inside her thrashed furiously.

"My daughter," Robert finally said. "She's here."

He would introduce them, he promised. He would do the right thing.

All her life Tiffany had wished not to be an only child. Her father knew this, which made the situation that much crueler.

"The fuck, Dad. If I told Mom that I were having a baby." This was a recurring nightmare of hers, confessing an unplanned pregnancy. She'd never imagined it would be a pregnancy like this.

They were seated in a lavish Peking duck restaurant, where she couldn't cause a scene or even raise her voice. She hadn't wanted to come tonight. She was sick of rich foods and her father's attentions, the way he watched her so carefully, like a child fearful of punishment.

"It was an accident," he said. As if that excused him. As if this kind of stuff happened all the time.

Well, maybe it did. Mistresses were common here, weren't they? *Xiao san*, little thirds, modern-day concubines. Her father, though? Where did he get the money, the nerve, the stamina?

Duck fat coated her tongue, a tasteless film of grease coagulating in the back of her throat.

"She wants to meet you."

"Why?"

"For the baby. For family." He lowered his head, chastened

by her glare. "Lunar new year is coming up. I hope you'll give her a chance."

"How did you—" She ran through the places where mistresses might prowl. Massage parlors. Bathhouses. Gross. Maybe she was just some mousy secretary. "Nevermind. I don't want to know."

"She's really nice."

"Dad. Please."

Tiffany waited for something like an apology—repentance—but there was none.

"You're grown up now," he said. "You know your parents are just people, too. We make mistakes. We're not perfect."

"No one asked you to be perfect. Keeping it in your pants is a far cry from perfect."

They left most of the food uneaten, walking back toward the subway station in silence. Cars sped by beneath them as they crossed the skybridge. Squares of light glimmered in the canopy of buildings. For the first time since she arrived in Beijing, Tiffany felt a pang of homesickness, not for home in general but for some kind of cellar, a hiding place, her mother's closet. The rustle of skirts above her, a jumble of high heels and old running shoes behind her. Somewhere, far away, her father was counting to ten. For years now, she has successfully hid. She hid boyfriends and boys that were just hook-ups. She hid the few nights where she got too drunk, plus other nights where she experimented with drugs that showed up at parties. Just marijuana and E, nothing major. She hid her new prescription, which helped with those deep, desolate days when she didn't want to get out of bed.

Wasn't life easier when they were hiding? Why had he pulled her into his bullshit?

Before they parted ways at the station, her father managed to recover enough paternal instinct to make demands of her again.

"Come to the house for New Year's. It'll be good for everyone." And then, "Don't say anything to Mom, okay? I'll talk to her."

Her stomach sank even before the escalator began to lower her into the tunnel.

"You know." She turned to look back at her father. "She must have some seriously sad story, your new friend. Why else would she stick it out with you?"

Tiantian followed her grandmother's steps for making the dough and dumpling filling. Back home in the countryside, her mother would soon be doing the same, mincing cabbage, ginger, pork; frying up ribbons of sweet dough so the younger generation in the village could crunch on her famed *mahua*.

Tiantian didn't call often, but it was the new year.

"You sent a lot of money," her mother said. "I don't need that much."

"Get yourself something nice or save it if you can't bring yourself to spend it. I got a nice bonus this year."

"You work so much. You can't take a break to come visit?"

"American companies, you know. They don't celebrate our New Year."

"If you're so busy, when will you have time to find a husband?"

"What do I need a husband for? The boss likes my work. I might get a raise soon."

Her mother sighed. "I can make some *mahua*, ship them out to you."

"Don't tire yourself. By the time they get here, they'll be stale."

Tiantian folded the dumplings herself. With each one she sealed, she resolved to hold tighter to this life she had stirred up. The baby inside her kicked. Robert's *gurou*. His bone, his flesh. The same cut as his daughter's. Didn't this baby deserve just as much? A happy childhood, a chance to go to school, to build a life of their own choosing?

The girl showed up just shy of seven, two hours late. "I thought it was dinner," she said.

Tiantian assured her that all was fine, no need to be polite. After all, it was family, not outsiders.

She studied the girl hungrily, drinking in each detail of her face. There was Robert's nose and brow, but the lips and jaw were someone else's, more delicate. Pretty. Her hair hung loose and messy over her shoulders, streaked with coppery highlights. She wore no jewelry or makeup, and her oversized sweater hung shapelessly down to her knees. She made no effort to hide her displeasure. She was insolent and rude, but she ate with exquisite care, taking small bites and never parting her lips as she chewed.

Tiantian could copy her poise but not that other thing, that Americanness. Tiffany was not burdened by worry or guilt. She acted in a way that was only possible when you were assured of your own safety. Of your worth.

Would her child learn these same Western ways? Robert had started looking at schools, not in America but here, where plenty of ex-pats worked as teachers, he said. He could pay the expensive tuitions and also tutor the child at home, ensure he would grow up prepared to attend universities abroad. Harvard or MIT.

Tiantian had learned some English when she first started hostessing, to better attract western patrons. She'd select a few phrases to practice during each shift. After she met Robert, he bought her language-learning apps and helped her study so she could apply for different jobs that would put her into a better career. He made introductions and helped her select a suit jacket for interviews. When those jobs turned out to pay less than what she made before, she gave up looking and he didn't push her. Perhaps he liked the idea that he could provide everything she needed.

Now she studied to make herself a suitable mother. She downloaded podcasts full of stilted English conversations and stole two books from an ex-pat café. One cover featured a cowboy and a woman in a torn red dress; the other one an ancient Roman coin. She got a notebook and wrote down each new vocabulary word.

When the girl switched to English, Tiantian could understand little bits.

"Did you talk to Mom yet?" the girl wanted to know.

Robert said he'd been too busy. Work was exceedingly stressful.

"But it's a holiday."

Robert switched back to Mandarin. "The holiday doesn't really start till next week. I'll be home by then."

This was also his home though, and this was the day they would share together for new year's, so Tiantian insisted on a family photo. She set her phone on Robert's desk and started the timer. Robert raised a freshly cooked dumpling into the air, but the skin ripped. Hot oil spilled onto his lap, followed by the nugget of meat. The camera managed to capture both his frank astonishment and Tiffany's grim smile.

Tiantian made the best of it. "So cute," she said. "I will print copies."

Later, when she and Tiffany were in the kitchen, she tested her English. "You miss your mom?"

The girl shrugged.

"I miss my mom."

The girl looked genuinely sympathetic. "I'm sorry. Did you lose her pretty young?"

Tiantian shrugged. Easy enough to let people believe what they wanted. She'd never corrected Robert on that same assumption. "Is good she does not see that I am scoundrel."

"Well, that's kind of harsh." The girl took a plate from her and began drying it. "I mean, we all make bad choices."

The girl seemed to soften, and Tiantian wondered what kind of bad choices she was imagining. She didn't want the girl's pity. Pity could only be played one way—make yourself sadder and smaller until you could no longer stand on your own. Sweet girl, sad girl, helpless, regrettable.

She made herself smile, adding a touch of conspiracy to her voice. "Are you scoundrel?"

"I'm lying to my mother."

"So we are scoundrel sisters."

"Actually, I'm sister to that one," Tiffany corrected, pointing to the belly. "But age-wise, nothing makes sense."

"I hope that one not scoundrel."

"You should maybe find a different word."

"You help teach me English?"

The girl didn't like that suggestion. She set the plate down. It clattered against the counter. "Look. We're not actually family."

Then she left to join her father in front of the television. Tiantian finished cleaning in the kitchen.

When Spring Festival arrived, she was alone all day in the apartment. Firecrackers thundered across the city. After a sleepless night, she stepped out in the early morning, walked abandoned streets littered with torn red paper. Storefronts were shuttered as migrants returned to the countryside and locals ventured out on vacation. She lost herself in the quiet morning fog, walking aimlessly for hours while running through vocabulary lists in her mind. Brawn, bronze; disheveled, shovel. The movement lulled the baby to sleep inside her, and each word she conjured was like an incantation to guard the child and project to it pleasant dreams. The least she could do while they still shared her body.

Lan had always credited herself with a sixth sense for disaster. Many women had it. Intuition, they called it in the U.S. Hers was different. Hers was an inheritance from the women in her bloodline who had watched their husbands wracked by opium, their children hunted by the Japanese, their riches burned or pillaged by the Communists and the Kuomingtang. Generations of misfortune had taught her how to sense imminent peril.

Naturally, she thought first of her daughter. At a dinner with family friends, she cornered Tiffany's confidante and asked all the leading questions. She knew how to find her way in. A few compliments and some light discussion of college life, then a rapid interrogation about drugs, alcohol, mental health, sexual behavior. By the time she was done, the girl couldn't form a coherent sentence. Lan had gathered nothing useful.

When her husband returned, she peppered him with questions, trying to uncover every detail about her daughter's life in Beijing. So preoccupied with this task, she failed for weeks to take note of her husband's unwarranted cheerfulness. He walked around the house, humming—old Chinese ballads from the '80s, a children's song their daughter used to sing about washing her white handkerchief. The praise came showering down, too. How she flavored the pork just right. How sharp she looked in her green blouse. Yet he made no overtures in the bedroom. So, he had taken a lover. She hoped he did not embarrass himself. How a man his age must exert himself to keep a lover. A costly endeavor, too. She completed a thorough review of their finances, but found nothing amiss. She wondered how much he'd stashed away in some Chinese bank she couldn't access.

She meted out her punishment in small doses. A raw spicy pepper hidden beneath a slice of beef in the bowl she served him. A small slit to the garbage bag before he took it outside. She waited to start the laundry only after he had jumped into the shower. Although the house was too big for her to hear his yelp of surprise when the water turned ice cold, she still found satisfaction in it.

Yet her right eye continued to twitch in anticipation of the danger she could not see.

"Don't eat from any street stalls," she told her daughter whenever Tiffany deigned to pick up her call. "Don't ride in any black cabs. If the driver kidnaps you, no one would ever know."

"Oh my god, Mom. There are way wealthier kids they could kidnap."

But she had two healthy kidneys, a fertile or yet to be proven otherwise womb, and a pleasant enough face. Her life was full of riches she took for granted, though she'd only get mad if Lan mentioned this.

She should have checked her husband's phone sooner. She'd been generous not to. It only took three attempts to crack the password. The year Tiffany was born. Finding the evidence was harder. She'd never used WeChat before.

The girl was very pretty. Big eyes and long black hair, no dyes or highlights. A traditional sort. Robert looked ridiculous next to her, his broad smile an assault. Lan burned with shame on his behalf. This was just the photo on her profile, but there were so many more. Years and years of infidelity. A relationship. Lan scrolled through the assault of photos to the very bottom, as if that would reveal how it all began.

She could see the girl becoming bolder, a hand latched onto his arm, a teasing photo with her tongue out. God, she was so young. The real secret came out. A topless photo with her hand cupped coyly around the small swell of belly. Lan didn't like to see others so exposed, not in the way that it laid yourself bare, too. At the sonogram image, a distant heartbeat came thudding into her ears. Her own, it turned out. Then, the image that stopped her heart entirely.

Her daughter, seated at the table with her father and his mistress. In the photo, Robert had yet to recover from the surprise of getting caught, and Tiffany wore a callous smile, looking directly, it seemed to Lan, at her, laughing at her foolishness.

The belly continued to grow. It reached the point of grotesque and kept going. Tiantian no longer wanted to be seen in public with it. Shame roiled through her, hot as heartburn, unbearable. In a moment of stupid weakness, she called Bella, who rushed over all too happily.

While her friend had bubbled over with reassurances when the baby was a speck, a mere notion, she was now full of foreboding.

"How could he leave you in this state?" she cried. "Not a man to be trusted out there. Worthless. Good thing I'm here for you."

And that was how Bella moved in. She was a messy roommate. She brought her business with her, one or two guys a week. Tiantian could hear them from her bedroom, but it was always over in a few hours. Worse was how much talking Bella did when she wasn't working. She had a Zhang Ailing quote for everything, which she'd recite in an even more supercilious register.

On all the new girls Kai was hiring at the KTV: "So you are young? So what? In two years, you will be old."

After Tiantian ended a call with Robert, she cast a sidelong gaze: "A man will never love a woman he thoroughly understands."

When Tiantian's irritation finally broke through: "She grew angrier and angrier. Then she had a child."

Without any solicitation, Bella offered up all kinds of solutions and strategies for imaginary scenarios. Hold the baby hostage and demand a gift every time Robert wanted to visit. A cash gift, of course. Nothing better than cash, except an education. Get Robert to send him to one of the private international schools. Get him to pay for her own education. Learn something new, something on computers.

As Bella went on about her friend's sister's business venture into computer vision glasses, Tiantian's phone buzzed with a WeChat ID she did not know. The profile photo was the standard gray silhouette.

The message: *I am Robert's wife. It is time we talk.*

She shut her phone before Bella could catch anything amiss.

Gathering her composure, she stopped the other woman mid-sentence. "You've been so kind to stay here with me, but I shouldn't trouble you anymore. Robert will be back soon. I want to have the place ready for him."

Bella's face turned as guarded as a walnut's shell. "We've known each other a long time, haven't we?"

Tiantian nodded. "You're a good friend."

"I helped you. I got you a good job. You've had it easy, but a child is a serious matter. There's no limit to what a child can take from you."

"You're not wrong, but a child can also bring life's greatest reward." She could have sworn Bella had told her as much, earlier on. "I'm a mother now. I have to make different choices, wiser choices. I have to be careful the company I keep."

And that was how Bella moved out.

The silence that stretched into the space felt infinite. The apartment was a prison, her body a different prison. There was no one else in the world who could come break the silence, so heavy it threatened to drown her. She couldn't rise against it and sat with her back against the wall as night fell and darkness pooled around her.

So many times, she had tried to ask Robert about his plan for the future. Any plan. He seemed to think they would simply continue as they had been, except now with a child.

Her mother had asked her to visit again. Or, if work was too busy, then maybe she could take the train to the city. She could travel with a friend.

A child wanted so much.

Her phone juddered next to her on the floor, some random alert lighting up the screen. This was enough to spur her to action.

Even though Lan had written in Chinese, Tiantian used a dictionary to compose her message in English.

My father died young, leaving me and my very poor mother. We worked hard but received little wages. Life is difficult for a woman. You are pushed always to be stuck. As a woman yourself, you must understand me. Will you find it in your kind heart to lend a helping hand? Can you do it yourself to drag someone out of her struggle?

After Lan picked up her daughter from the airport, Tiffany seemed to sense her displeasure and thus desire her closeness. It was like when she misbehaved as a child, needy for affection after a timeout or a scolding. Instead of going to bed as she should, Tiffany requested a movie—whatever Lan wanted to watch—and sidled close to her on the couch. Lan could not get comfortable. China had stained her daughter. Even after her shower, she smelled polluted.

Later, she wanted to climb into bed with her. "Just for awhile," she said. "Maybe I'll get sleepy. It's not like Dad's here."

Robert had returned to China two weeks ago, blissfully ignoring Lan's coldness toward him.

"Do you miss him when he's not here?"

"Who? Your dad?"

Tiffany nodded. Only her head poked out from under the covers. Her eyes looked bleary.

"I'm used to it. When you've been married for so long, some separation is helpful. Everyone lives their own lives."

"Aren't you ever curious? What he does with his life in China?"

"Should I be?"

She wanted her daughter to say it, to be on her side. It didn't matter to her, how Robert chose to live. She just didn't want her daughter to lie to her.

"No." The girl's voice was soft and miserable. "I don't know."

Tiffany had always preferred her father more.

"You sleep now," Lan said. "I have some work to finish up."

"I'm glad to be home," Tiffany added.

"Well, home is where you belong."

Downstairs, with her laptop glowing on the kitchen island and all the lights in her house turned off, Lan composed another message to her husband's mistress. Across the dark expanse of lawn, shadows moved over the lighted window shades of the neighbor's house. So many lives locked into each square of land. How odd, that the person she felt closest to lay across the ocean, in bed with her husband. Who else knew the topology of her husband's body? Who else knew the weight of his child, tucked against her bones? As she typed, affection rose from the pit of her stomach, something like gratefulness. Here was this person with whom no more secrets needed to be kept. Affection swiftly curdled with humiliation.

After hours of suffering the indignities of childbirth, straining and pushing to a room full of spectators, Tiantian submitted to the cesarean. Blinking from the surgical lights, her body shaking with cold, she tried to focus her vision on the small, purple mass the doctors placed on her chest. Its squealing cries reverberated through her.

"A boy," Robert said. "A big, healthy boy."

The nurses cooed over him, calling it little treasure, budding scholar. "Mom's still recovering," one of the nurses told Robert. "She must take great care during the convalescence month."

The labor was long. She was too tired to hold the baby, resentful when they tried to get him to latch to her.

"Bonding will come naturally," the nurse reassured them.

Robert could not request paternity leave for a secret child, and so his time off was limited. Tiantian requested a stay at a maternity hotel, where staff could cook the meals and care for the baby. "So precious," they said about the boy, but they were lying. The child did not look right to her. She spent hours searching his small, pimpled face for signs of intelligence, character, or warmth.

Eventually, his full-time care fell to her. She gave herself over to the child's unceasing needs. He was underweight and voracious, crying every few hours to be fed but unable to latch. Her milk, slow to come in, was quick to dribble out. Luckily, Robert had packed a suitcase full of baby formula from the U.S.

Awake in the night for feedings, she scrolled through articles about autism and sociopathy and birth defects related to paternal age or air pollution. What was not readily apparent now could take many more years to manifest. She had no doubt something was waiting to emerge from those tangled strands of DNA. All those coils and snares, a mess even before they unraveled, wrapping around her and knotting her into an untenable life.

For now, Robert was pleased, swearing a resemblance only he could see.

"Must be all the wrinkles," Tiantian said, feeling mean and knowing she could get away with it. She thought of Tiffany, fearless in her insolence, confident she would be loved and protected. How long would this be true for herself? She was no longer youthful, but used up. She needed to make plans accordingly.

The morning Robert left to complete the baby's citizenship paperwork at the U.S. embassy, to get all the proper stamps, Tiantian called Lan via WeChat while giving the baby a bottle.

"I'll take the money," Tiantian said.

Lan had proposed to buy her off in their last text exchange.

Now she seemed hesitant. "Really? Are you sure? No more contact. You've thought it through?"

Her *putonghua* was flawless, unaccented by country or city.

"I stand by my word," Tiantian promised. She would leave
Robert.

"He'll come after you. What will you do when he finds you?"

"He won't find me."

"How can you be so sure?"

"He thinks he knows China. He doesn't."

She would talk to Kai and ask for help. Kai had connections
across many cities and probably overseas as well. With the
money, she could sign up for proper classes somewhere. There
were endless paths one could take. So many paths and so many
people, it wasn't hard to cover one's tracks. The difficult part was
re-tracing those steps. You could only move on, move forward.
No looking back.

"The child," Robert's wife said. "What if he gets sick? What
if you need help?"

As if on cue, the baby began to fuss, letting out a mewling
cry as its tongue rooted for food. Tiantian shoved the tip of her
pinky between his lips.

"Haven't you thought it through?" Anger seized her throat.
She had run out of patience for people who had the luxury of
deliberating over their decisions. "This was your plan. Are you
so soft you'll let a crying baby break you?"

"The child's innocent. I don't want it to suffer."

"I'm glad to hear that." It was true. She hadn't expected such
relief. Perhaps the second part of her plan would succeed then,
the part that Lan did not know. "I'll take whatever amount is
enough to soothe your conscience."

"You can reach me, I suppose. If you really needed to."

"I won't. I plan to disappear completely."

"Am I doing the right thing?"

"That's not for me to say. But I will say thank you. This is what I want. What do you want?"

"I want you gone."

Tiantian confirmed the transactions and double-checked the amounts as she packed her suitcase. She would only take one bag to clear out of this borrowed space. There were only so many things for her to keep. When she finished, she gazed deeply into the baby's sleeping face, trying to see into the future the person he would become. In the end, she had to accept that this was a face she would never know.

Before she left, she sent one more message. *Scoundrel sister. I have left you a brother. Treat him nicely. Don't be too mean.*

Robert didn't think much of Tiffany's text, *everything okay?* He was still waiting for his number to be called, for his turn to go up to the window. When he bounded up the stairs back home, he was mostly thinking about dinner. He was ready to eat, to shower, to settle into the comfort of the couch. But the infant was crying in his playpen, his clothes soiled and his crumpled face red and sweaty. He turned about in search for Tiantian, a curse under his breath for her negligence. Then he froze, noting the open bureau doors and pillaged closet. He picked up the closest object, a pen, and held it in front of him as he prepared to approach her dead body. When he was certain she had left of her own accord, simply packed her things and walked away, he kicked the desk in rage and stubbed his toe. Finally, he changed and fed the baby.

In the years that followed, a tingling numbness would occasionally creep over his toes and remain there for days. Each time, humiliation seeped forward from the past, as fresh and fetid as in this moment now, sweat pooling in his armpits and at the small of his back.

His wife asked for a divorce when he returned home with the child. Before the papers went through, she discovered a lump in her left breast and accused him of bringing it about through the bitterness he had caused her. She stayed because she needed him. Over time, mutual guilt tempered mutual anger.

They told their friends they adopted the boy from distant relatives, recently deceased. He grew up healthy and gentle-spirited, never quite displaying the same quickness as Tiffany. Because of Tiantian's many assertions that the child was not right, Robert appraised him often for signs of disability. There appeared to be none, but he remained so watchful that he was significantly gratified when the child was placed in a remedial math class.

At eight years old, Albert Cao loved cars, Legos, and art. He did not like writing or subtracting. His favorite person in the world was his sister, who built the best Lego cars and who never studied him as if she were trying to measure up something inside him. He liked to draw pictures of his sister, his cars, and his mom, whom he had never met. His auntie said that his mother was not here because she had no heart, because wolves had eaten her heart. He did not believe her, because his sister told him this was not true. Then his sister had shown him his mother, on a narrow strip of photo paper. She was sitting at the dinner table, smiling broadly over a plate of dumplings. Albert asked if he could keep the photo, and Tiffany had let him.

DEAR VLAD

These days, everyone walked around in black leather or yellowed lace or red velvet. Everyone brushed on layers and layers of chalk-white face powder and implemented all varieties of dietary restrictions — paleo, raw, macrobiotic, micronutritious — just to capture that perfectly cadaverous sheen.

That, at least, was what I told Mummsies and Daddy-O when Vlad came to pick me up, all spiffed up with a red bowtie and what must have been a dry-clean only kind of cape.

"But what about that nice Steve Zimmerman?" Mummsies asked. "The one who plays water polo? He took you to homecoming?"

Her voice rose a pitch with every question.

Mums was third best cheerleader or something back when Miller was her high school. That's like working just as hard as the two best cheerleaders but still getting stuck on all fours at the bottom left of the pyramid with someone's knee jabbing your spine. As third best cheerleader, you dated linebackers, never the quarterback. Daddy was one of the linebackers. He didn't get it, either. "For Pete's sake, Cate, you're an honor roll student," he said when I started painting my nails black.

It was a quick Dad-meet-Vlad. The fatherly heft quivered in consternation, doling out the requisite warnings. The maternal unit didn't even bother snapping photographs. She adjusted my corsage of black roses, fingers lingering as if she were trying to charm the blooms back into color.

Her dejection made her quite lovely. Typically, she's got this deranged grimace-grin—the root cause of her tension headaches? It couldn't be good to hold your expression that way, but I suppose that's how years of cheerleading from the bottom-left will leave you. Her face so downtrodden now, I wanted to pat her silly head. I did. The emotions came.

Here I was, all grown up, about to wander off into the night with a guy once nicknamed the Impaler—plans in place they wouldn't even think to interrogate. There they were, doltishly holding hands, framed by the front door and the foyer light. Later, they would wash up dishes, watch the telly, and maybe play a round of Scrabble or maybe not before they headed to bed, innocent as rabbits. It was just so sad.

I almost chickened then, but I couldn't. I had made a pact.

Join up with Vlad—and we would get our friend back. Best friends forever. We were the BFs. Vlad offered the forever.

Annabel was the brains behind this one. "Imagine what we could *do* with an eternity," she said.

Britt thought it was genius. "We'd go everywhere. All across the world. We'd take London by storm, wouldn't we?" She turned my direction, knowing how much I longed to cast aside our small Midwestern town for Westminster Abbey and the chimes of Big Ben.

Britt hadn't needed to goad me. I was never one for getting left behind.

We picked black and red as our colors. I wore a strapless sequined red tube top and a black tutu skirt. My curls I pinned in place with black butterfly clips. I'd been wild about the clips, but they were plastic and felt childish now. Annabel's blonde hair was coiled at her nape and adorned with a single white rose. For the dress, she'd gone an oriental route with this crimson silk piece that seemed prim and proper at first, a trail of cloth buttons winding up to her neck, but then you noticed the leg slits rising to mid-thigh and the lustrous fabric hugging all the other parts above that. Dark lace gloves rolled up to her elbows were the finishing touch. Britt's black jumpsuit had a plunging neckline and billowing pantlegs cropped slightly above her sparkling ruby slippers. Her long braids gathered into a thick ponytail hung down past her waist to the belt of red poppies, black feathers, and silvery twine brambles—a Britt original. Little combs brandishing ruby droplets glistened along her temples.

Outside Miller High, we all squeezed together in the backseat of the limo and snapped a Polaroid. Vlad marveled as our image seeped into the white square around his own blank shape, which resisted such modern wonders and also mirrors.

We made a decently stunning tableau. If Darla were still with us, she would have outshined us all. She'd always had that aura. So cold. So darling.

Darla found Vlad on the Internet. Exclusive classifieds. You had to have loads of money or a rare hereditary condition—preferably both—in order to sign on. Of Vlad, she wrote in her diary, *Recluse, not loner. Yearns for the whirl and rush of humanity. Seeks communion with body _and_ mind. Total cognitive connection.* "I want to share your life, your change, your death, all that makes you what you are."

Britt decided that this gave him depth. Not your average vampire predator.

"Yeah," I said, "because he's the OG vampire predator."

"More time and more people to malign him," Britt said, as if he were simply misunderstood.

"He needs us, too," Annabel declared.

I tried to posit tactfully which things he might really need. Like, how many liters of blood were we talking about? But the plan was already hatched. From the back corner of the library, we found a few good photos of ourselves and sent them along with a pleading note to thegreatdracul@hotmail.com.

He responded within hours, attaching a self-portrait saved as a PDF. White and red oil pastels swirled together against a black background to make a smirking face. In person, though, he had quite a few nice features: deep dimples, dark brows, a decisive widow's peak. He spoke of Darla with fondness. Moreover, he spoke of Darla with mutability. She was not a closed book with a sad ending. She was healing and gathering strength, adapting and training. She was, in a word, busy. Much too busy to come back for prom.

So maybe we only believed what we wanted to believe. Maybe we were gullible little girls who ought to stay off the Internet. Maybe we were old enough to know better.

But, reader, what would you do if you spent months watching your best friend die, her fierce will whittled away by another bad scan and an unlikely infection, until her only hope was a name that haunted her lips, a dark name she whispered over and over.

Suppose you spent most of that time thinking the drugs had made her delusional. After the funeral you went to her grave with your friends, the three of you slipping out after dark, and you saw her tombstone just as she said it would be, cracked right down the middle. You saw the overturned earth, still soft and fresh, and you knew that if you dug all day and night, you would reach that burnished mahogany coffin, but you couldn't be sure anymore whether or not she was still inside, because shadows shift in a quiet graveyard and that rustle of movement could be anything—human or animal or half-animal half-human or spirit or nothing at all. When the three of you sat down around the Ouija board—because you just wanted to talk once more, to know that she was safe, wherever her conclusion took her, an ending that was not happy but at least painless, you hoped—and the pull of the planchette spelled out that same dark name, and the wind whispered it too, and was it wind that tugged your hair or was it she? Did she send the beetles and the earthworms, or did so many of them always squirm out from newly turned dirt, inching toward the numbers on the spirit board?

What would you think if, not long after that, a terrible storm blew through—meteorologists flummoxed by clouds they couldn't name? *Came out of nowhere*, they said. No idea what it'd do next.

Next came the bats. Animal Control blamed the attacks on unusual weather patterns. They advised keeping cats and dogs indoors. The stations got hold of a reel of someone's pastures, and for weeks, local news offered up countless replays of cows slumped in the field, anemic from bats that latched onto their broad backsides.

When you visited your dead best friend's mother, a bouquet of daisies tucked under your arm, she was out on the back patio kneeling over your dead best friend's dead pet dog. "The damnedest thing," she kept murmuring, stroking the bassetoodle's matted white fur. Poor Lola. The puncture wounds were right below the purple collar, two deep red holes, the fur smeared pink all around them.

At night when you tried to sleep, a spate of bats would knock against your window, thud after thud, so loud you wondered if they were dropping unconscious into your backyard. You wondered how many pills your parents were taking each night, sleeping through this ruckus? You cower under the covers, bury your head under the pillow. You try your best to ignore them because you know that once you open a window to Vlad, God closes the door.

The bats began to bring us gifts. The white ribbon she wore in her hair. An opal button from her favorite designer frock. White lilies like the ones from her memorial service. How could we refuse them? How could we refuse her?

We let them drink from the hollows of our elbows. The bruises alone brought us closer to her, our violet welts resembling the ones inside her elbows, down her arms, and along her legs. The sting of our veins breaking eased as bite after successive bite numbed the initial burn. The bats came to us every night. As they drank, our minds swirled and spun, filling with the same vision.

Prophecies, Annabel called them. *Temptation*, Britt proposed. I thought they were more like warnings, but I knew we wouldn't heed them.

Darla was calling to us inside those dreams. As always, we couldn't resist her.

I'd seen it all before, the dance floor in the high school gymnasium shimmering into my dreams like an underwater kingdom. I'd always wondered why a green figure in a leotard sashayed by, trailing confetti through my dreams. It turned out that our esteemed prom committee had selected the theme of Lake

Enchantment, and the drama kids were only too eager to prance around as wood and water nymphs.

The nightmare began with prom. Britt and Annabel whirled out of my reach, past the basketball hoop/maypole, swept into the throng of bodies. I'd follow them anywhere, but I wasn't setting one foot into that soup of sweat, pheromones, and shit perfume.

So many nights, I had wandered down empty hallways lined with metal lockers, threading my way toward the exit. I couldn't have veered from this path if I wanted to. A circle of boys hid in the stairwell, drinking their contraband beer. Welcome to the Miller High Life. I ignored them and headed to the second floor. Here, the music faded away except for the bass landing an occasional punch to my gut. Soon, I was standing in front of her locker.

The combination was still the same. The door swung open with the tiniest of creaks. Otherworldly mustiness wafted over me — the last twinges of her floral shampoo, released from the dust and mote with which it had been locked up for over half a year. A few faded paper flowers lay crumpled in the corner. For a while her locker had been a shrine, candles and wreaths and handwritten notes worked through the slots as if some postal worker would pick them up and ferry them down the Styx. I guess someone had collected them, eventually. I wondered what they'd done with it all.

It was amazing how many people wanted to write to her, how many people had things to tell her, their emotions too big to contain so they had to shed it off to someone who was already gone. They weren't friends to her when she was alive. They didn't even really know her. One nosedrip of a girl actually came up to us once, to let us know that Darla's ill-begotten fate was all in God's hands, and He was master of one grand plan, and heaven had gained another angel. Little did she know. Darla gave up on heaven a long time ago.

Admit it. When you picture her, you go the cherubic route, too. Don't you? Blonde and frail and guileless. Big-eyed innocence. Sick kids are always made to be saints, like they're too good to exist in this world or something.

Darla may have looked the part, but she carried wickedness in her bones. When she wanted to, she could make grown men cry. She could turn her eyes to steel and see exactly how to break a person. After Vice Principal Chao gave her a two-month detention where she spent homeroom hour in his office, his hair went totally gray before the end of her sentence. When the handsy swim coach stopped Annabel too many times after practice, Darla made sure everybody knew about his sperm count problem, which may or may not have been a real problem, but what did that matter? Rumors spread, the man lost his mojo and stopped flirting with both teachers and students—his personal swim squad benched.

Darla was cruel and crafty, and we were so grateful to have her on our side. She was like the hardest metal in the world. Nothing could cut her, because nothing was worse than what her own dark materials had already wrought. That was the secret to her power.

But her darkness, repressed for years, came back hungrier than ever. The only thing that could cure her was a total replacement of all the cells, tissue, and brackish matter that lived inside her marrow. The transplant worked for nearly two years. Then, it didn't. A creature had formed inside her and would no longer submit to her control. It nibbled at her liver, her kidneys, her spleen. She crumbled from the inside out.

There was nothing we could do but watch.

I placed our Polaroid onto the top shelf of her locker, where her lunch and her U.S. History textbook used to go. An offering to her, perhaps, wherever she was. A clue for someone else to find, after we were gone.

When the door shut, it clanged with finality. I couldn't quite articulate what it was I was saying goodbye to, but I ached for it just as much as I ached for her.

He was waiting for us in the limo, ready to take us to our next destination.

As we sped past the road that led homeward, my heart lurched for my parents. I hoped they were laying down Scrabble tiles and counting up points, arguing over which letters constituted a word. If in fact I never returned home, I hoped their sadness eased quickly. They never really learned how to talk about their feelings, those two, but bless them, they did try. Countless conversations on the edge of my bed, long pauses punctuated by major-league throat-clearing, always wrapped up with an awkward pat on my shoulder or a tousling of my hair. Perhaps they would meet their daughter's disappearance with the same stalwart nature. I hoped so. I hoped they moved on quickly, retired early, traveled, found new hobbies.

Before I realized it, we were already there, the west entrance of Renfield Cemetery.

Darla's grave was in the northeast corner, past the Renfield family mausoleum touting its large crucifix, upon which a most tortured Christ figure writhed, frozen, against his eternal agony.

Tonight, his wide stone eyes seemed to follow us in a panic, mouth gaping in admonishment rather than anguish.

A full moon lit our path. I followed Britt who followed Annabel who followed Vlad, our new leader. Down the slope of thick wild grass. Around the flooded gulch, where a toddler's shoe lay waiting inside the murky water. Walking past the thick blackberry brambles along the west wall, I sucked in a breath as a thorn sliced down the back of my hand.

Vlad stopped so abruptly that Annabel stumbled right into him. He didn't care. His gaze was on me. His eyes flashed with something like lightning. His tongue darted over those thin lips. Suddenly, he looked older to me, worn and decrepit, the veneer of youth wilting. His thin nostrils flared. Cringing under his hungry gaze, I brought my hand to my mouth and quickly licked away the trail of red beads. He smiled, suddenly back to normal, cheery as anything. He waved for us to hurry.

How long do you have to be missing before they start looking for you? I suppose it depends on who you are. If you wear black nail polish, they assume you're a runaway even if your parents insist you were a star student, never gave anyone any trouble. Eventually, they'll find our Polaroid and print our last-seen image onto newspapers, milk cartons, coupons. flyers. Maybe one day, you'll see us, smiling out at you from some bulletin board in a laundromat or a church basement. Maybe you'll see him, too, swallowing up the space where we are not. If you see our done-up faces, will you pity us, or will you think, deep down, that we got what we deserved. Or perhaps you won't even notice us. Your gaze will sweep right past us as you get on with your day — the endless errands, the sacred schedule, the same old same old.

Maybe it's best that we don't register. If we become his creatures, his jackals, maybe you shouldn't look for us at all. Maybe you should stay far, far away. We could turn you dangerous, unable to ignore our siren call, to the point where you forget your husband, leave your children, blow up your whole worthless life in pursuit of us.

A weeping angel with granite tears helmed Darla's new gravestone. The church replaced the one that cracked and added the statuette at no charge. Darla's dad recounted this kindness with stupefied amazement. We hoped she wasn't trapped beneath, squirming in discontent. We didn't know whether she would rise up from below to come claim us, her eager handmaidens. We only knew that Vlad would bring us here, to her.

Truth be told, this was where the visions ended. We had no idea what would happen next. Looking around at the dear faces of my best friends, I tried to repress a laugh. It was too bizarre that we were standing around wondering what to do, like any other Saturday night. I pictured us drinking each other's blood, painting our nails with it, braiding each other's hair and then settling back into donut-shaped floaties as blood saturated the pool beneath us.

Just when I thought I'd tamped down the giggles, Britt let out a snort, shoulders shaking with silent laughter. That did me in. I clutched my stomach as laughter racked me. Annabel stood ramrod straight, trying to hold it together, but the corners of her lips were quivering. She was almost at the edge, and then down she tumbled, on her knees bent over with laughter. The sound of her guffaws made me laugh so hard I cried. Through my blurred vision, the stone angel actually resembled Darla, giving me an impish wink.

Vlad called us back to attention. His presence was like a flash of lightning, his voice thundering through us. Our veins reverberated him. We knew his desire. We tasted his hunger.

At his beckoning, Annabel rose from the ground and floated trancelike to his side. With the glide of his long fingernail, Vlad released the trail of buttons from her throat to the side of her chest. His hand returned to her neck, stroking its pale length with one gnarled finger. Funny, that. His hands hadn't looked that way before.

Then there was his face, coming into focus just before he lowered it to Annabel's neck—a mottled clot of gnarled leather and bristles of fur. I turned to Britt, checking whether she had seen it, too. She stood there mesmerized but not repulsed, locked in a tranquil daze. Beyond her frozen figure, Darla waved.

She hopped off the granite block and behind her, the stone angel remained, still and silent.

"Hi there, Catey-Cakes," she said. "How's tricks?"

I tried to get the others' attention, but Vlad was speaking, his voice so loud inside my head, pulling me back in.

"Come on, Cate-Face. Give us a hug."

Her arms were as cold as ice, her skin alabastrine. I shivered at her touch. Together, we watched as Annabel's body jerked in some contorted dance. Her hair cascaded loose, the single white rose dropping to the earth.

"What do you think?" Darla said. "Is she made of sugar or spice?"

"Did he really bite?"

Her voice cut with scorn. "Stupid girl. What did you think was going to happen tonight?"

"We just wanted to be with you," I tried to explain.

She shook her head. "You didn't want to be without me."

"Isn't that the same thing?"

"You know it's not. And you know I can't save you. Look at me." She released her hold on my arm and spun me around. Now the earth was against my back. I sank into the soft dirt of her grave and her body hovered over me. "I'm a bag of bones. I'm meat salad."

To illustrate, she unlaced the top of her white shift and pulled apart the fabric to reveal a nest of vermin crawling and twitching in the cradle of her ribs. "You wouldn't believe how much this tickles."

One brown slug began to inch its way up her hand. She slurped it into her mouth, swallowed contentedly.

"What about —" I glanced toward Vlad, whose own rot was seeping down the sides of his widow's peak.

She rolled her eyes. "Honestly, kind of a loser. So full of himself. If I hear one more time about his great impaling."

The haughty tone engendered familiarity and an unexpected grief welled up in me. But then she turned her contempt toward me.

"What? Tears now? Isn't this what you wanted?"

She pressed closer. Her breath made my insides shrink.

"Poor little Cate-Face." Her crooning whispers chafed. "Scared of college. Scared of boys. Scared to grow up even though you get the chance to. Why would you think I had the ability or desire to save you?"

Her words stung, but they were true. Having never faced any substantial challenge, I was afraid of everything. Most of all, I was scared of being alone.

Graduation was looming. College after that. We weren't ready. After losing Darla, the three of us didn't want to part ways. We wanted to rewind time and stop it for good in the peak days of summer when we were all washed in a solstice glow, burgeoning with life and laughter.

"Don't you know you can never go back, Cate?" she asked, reading my mind. "And if you're stuck like me, you can't go forward, either. Is that what you want? Are you so scared that's all you know to want?"

"I want—" I started but couldn't continue. The vastness of the world engulfed me, drowned me in its immensity. I couldn't begin to comprehend it, much less grasp what I wanted of it. In the end, I settled back to what I knew. "I want you."

She screeched, surrounding me with her fury. It enveloped me, trembling against my skin until I could feel its trill inside me, as if I were screaming, too. I felt her rage, her helplessness, and somewhere inside it all, a strand of her light.

She felt me then, too, trying to pluck out the frayed threads of the Darla I knew. She swerved from me. The earth shifted beneath me, giving way as she pushed me down further into her grave. My body throbbed with her anger. I writhed inside her pain. My hands clawed against the dirt, desperate for an escape or a place to hide. My hands closed against something rough and solid, a jagged root. Her voice thundered inside me. "You'd trade your one life for this? Is that all you're good for?"

My body quaked with her voice. I could feel it threatening to crack. I tugged at the root, hoping to hoist myself away from here. The root snapped off. I had no choice. Darla lunged. I thrust the jagged stake between her breasts.

Silence. Such relief. We both sighed, simultaneously. The

faintest of smiles teased her lips. Her hand reached up and brushed my cheek, the gentlest touch before her dust shimmered and settled over me.

The air rippled in her absence. My chest vaulted with emptiness. But there was no time to grieve. I dug my fingers into the tufts of grass and damp earth to hoist myself up. In my other hand, Darla had left me her final gift—a small glass vial of holy water.

The night ended, like all eventful nights in Small Town, Ohio, at the 24-hour Steak 'n Shake. Repelled by holy water, Vlad had transformed into the largest, scraggliest bat I'd ever seen, briefly eclipsing the moon in his flight. We hiked back across the cemetery, past the tormented Christ, down the dark streets, until someone gave us a ride in his pickup truck and told us we should stop doing drugs. As the sky turned from dark to light blue, we wolfed down double-patty double-cheese steakburgers and chicken-fried chicken fingers. We had never been so hungry before in all our lives.

Picture us—smeared with dirt in our ripped dresses, mascara running down our cheeks. We did our best to clean up in the restroom, wiping off Annabel's dried blood with paper towels. Nobody asked questions. Out by its lonely stretch of the freeway, this establishment had seen a lot.

The fluorescent lights seemed brighter than before. I could feel their electric buzz pulsing inside me. I tried to ease the hum of energy, running my greasy fingers up and down the red vinyl seats.

I was the only one to have seen her. The others were caught up inside his web, suffocated by his will.

"But where did she go?" Annabel asked. "Did she fly off, too?"

I shook my head. "She's gone. She didn't want to go, but she had to."

I believed now that the visions we received were from Darla herself, calling for us to come save her. She'd granted us an epilogue, given us one more adventure. In return, she'd found a way to revise her own story.

"She must be somewhere still," Britt said. "People like her, they don't just fade away."

"Never," I said. "We won't let her."

Whatever we chose to do, however we chose to live, we would always come back together to remember her. She had dreamed futures on our behalf. Inside Darla's rage, I'd found that thread of light and within it, all her blessings for us.

Annabel, already accepted into a top liberal arts college, would rule at an influential law firm. Multinational corporations would topple under her scrutiny. She moved billions of dollars with her pen and her detailed note-taking. Eventually, after the law lost its luster, she'd adopt two little boys, and a gangly middle-aged one, too.

Britt followed each passionate affair with another, leaving a trail of scandal in her wake. She would be known for dismantling celebrity nuptials and toppling the economic and political structure of small well-to-do countries. Men and women alike feared what her advances could steal from them, but her heart would always remain pure.

As for me, the one who never liked to be left behind, I'd take off on my own to wander the streets of my beloved London, sipping Earl Grey, browsing old bookstores, and minding the gap. I would encounter all sorts of people, among them poets, artists, and the ghosts of dead musicians. They would come to me lonely and afraid, beseech me to join them, to caress their hair and soothe their hurts. I would offer them all that I could, but not everything, never more.

Maybe one of those people will be you, ghost or poet, or maybe none of this will happen and nothing is ever true. You choose what to believe, but just know that we are coming, into whatever future awaits us, thrumming with possibility and entropy. Maybe one day you'll take the seat next to us on the bus or walk past our booth in a fluorescent lit diner, watch us tear the last bits of meat off a chicken bone, or some other kind of animal. You won't know it's us. We'll burn the photograph.

Annabel raised her milkshake. "To the best one of us all," she said.

Britt clinked it against her Frappuccino. "The first to go, the last to be forgotten."

"To Darla," I said, and we sipped.

The sun rose over the horizon, the promise that time would continue its slow march forward. Golden light streaked through the gaps in the clouds. No matter where time took us, we would come back together to remember her. This was the small bit of immortality we could offer.

WE LIVED LIKE ASTRONAUTS

Carson searched the Internet and ordered six air plants. They sit with roots exposed inside clear glass eggshells — green ferns crinkled like a bad perm job and succulents shaped like roses. We hang two of them from the curtain rods and the rest from hooks on the ceiling.

There is a crack in the corner of the ceiling and sometimes bits of plaster rain down on our bedroom-living-room-dining-room. This studio is all of the above. A three-for-one, we call it. Plenty of room for two.

The trick to living in a small square footage is to embrace your vertical space. What you don't have in length and width, you make up for in height. Multiply it up and that's how you get volume.

In addition to the air plants, we buy floating shelves and hanging lights. We line up our knives on a magnetic strip and glue more magnets to the back of our spice tins so they can sit against the fridge. This is utility. If we had a ladder, we would build bookshelves along the upper edge of our walls. It would feel like we lived at the bottom of a very tall library, and we were very small.

I lost three boxes of books to the U.S. Postal Service. Somewhere in Iowa or Montana or Idaho are my copies of *Jane Eyre*, *Moby*

Dick, and the complete Austen. I like to think that they arrived on the doorstep of an unsuspecting teen girl growing up in the Bible belt, someone who has read only the God-breathed words of Christ. I picture my books emanating the warm glow of untapped temptation. In reality, they are probably still stacked in their boxes, buried underneath other boxes in a dank and unlit storage unit, a department of lost dreams. I imagine them cold and water damaged, shriveled pages starving for the touch of fingertips.

Carson tells me to look on the bright side. He is a firm believer in the bright side, which is one of the reasons why I love him and why I am willing to move across the country to be with him. He says that now we have fewer things to get rid of.

The other trick to living in a small space is to just get rid of your things. Kick your habit of mindless consumerism. Don't let your possessions possess you!

Back in Iowa City, I lived with my aunt in her duplex three blocks from campus.

"Move west with me," Carson had said, while we sat around her mahogany drop-leaf table eating spaghetti and meatballs from mango-wood Pottery Barn plates. "I'll teach you how to glissade. That's French for sliding down mountains on your ass."

"What would I do out there? After sliding down all those mountains?"

"You could do anything. What would you do here?"

I didn't answer.

He took my hand. "In Seattle, there's no winter. And no cornfields, either. There are mountains and islands and fields of raspberries. Come on. Take a bet on me."

I realized he was serious. We celebrated by rolling across the sheepskin rug, almost knocking over an antique standing birdcage. My aunt has no birds, only birdcages. She is an example of someone Carson would describe as possessed by her possessions. She owns three sets of china, two leather couches, and six empty birdcages.

Here in Seattle, we have none of those things, but we have each other, and we have our air plants.

Carson says that this is plenty.

"We don't need to be loaded down with books. We have library cards!"

It can also be said that I love Carson in spite of his bright side.

One of the things you have to prepare for when you move into a small space with someone you love is the possibility—or absolute certainty—that you will fight. Here are some of the things you might fight about: closet space, washing dishes and whether said washed dishes are verifiably clean, the number of days post-expiration date that milk is safe to drink, curtains versus blinds, headache remedies, how fruit flies breed.

Carson and I could have fought about any one of those things, but we have worked through all of them by using I statements, compromise, and negative feedback loops that de-escalate emotional tension in a positive way.

What we do fight about is more difficult to define. It springs up from somewhere unknown and discolors everything that has come before.

"Are we only pretending to be nice?" I ask.

"I don't know what you're talking about. We're going to be late."

I put on one shoe but pause in front of the other. "If you don't want me to go, you shouldn't feel the need to invite me."

"Do you not want to go?" he asks, and then continues, "Why wouldn't you want to go? The party's on a boat."

Carson is thinking about balloons and beer and a boatful of friends. I am thinking about seasickness and silent looks and the lack of walls and exits.

"You really don't want to go?" he asks.

We are entering a positive feedback loop, which aggravates emotional distress in a negative way so that emotions grow further distressed.

I kick the shoe off my foot. "I just want to be with people who love me before they love you."

"My friends do love you."

"But they love you more."

"So what? They've known me longer."

"I just want someone who's on my side," I say.

"Since when are we picking sides?"

"I don't know." I'm confused because suddenly we are standing on opposite sides.

He crosses his arms. "Why would we need to pick sides?"

I think of an earthquake, a plague, a kickball game. Who would pick me to be on their side, if the earth cracked open beneath our feet?

"Now I don't want to go anymore, either." Carson sits down on the wooden chest we use for storage and seating.

"No, you should go. I'm fine here. I don't really like boats. It's nothing personal. I just didn't grow up near a body of water."

Carson goes for a walk, not to the boat. He does not invite me to come along.

I resolve not to dwell on this and, instead, move the wooden chest around the room so that I can stand on it as I spray the air plants with water. The correct term for this is misting. The air plants do not need soil or water to survive, only a delicate misting, every once in a while. It seems cruel to deny them their natural thirst, but they are not like other plants. They have learned another way to subsist.

When Carson comes back, he brings a ladder.

"Someone was just going to throw this away," he says.

We move the ladder to the middle of the room and stand it up like an inverted V. There are five metal rungs, and after I climb them I sit at the top and reach my hands up to touch the rough swirls of paint that swirl across our ceiling. From here, I can spray the air-plants without craning my neck and see each crinkly leaf on the ferns. Carson has a turn as well. He is taller and the fit is tighter, but he sits with his back straight and examines the walls.

The next day, he brings home long wooden planks that he smooths down with sandpaper. He nails metal supports high up on the walls and then secures the boards in place.

"Now we need some books," he says when he is done.

It is almost midnight, so we wait, admiring our book-shelves from our mattress on the ground, which feels a great distance away.

"I feel like we're ants," I whisper into his neck.

"Are ants super quiet?" he whispers back to me.

"They're the quietest."

He rolls up over me and shouts in my face, "Maybe we're astronauts. Who have to yell across space."

In outer space, astronauts are even smaller than ants. I swing him back down so that I am on top. "Houston, do you copy?"

"Roger that." He slides two fingers into my boxer shorts. "Have you ever wondered how astronauts have sex?"

"That's what I would do if I were in outer space. I would have sex with you."

His face turns serious. "Are you sad about your books? You should have books. You shouldn't change for me."

I answer with a kiss. "Are you sad you missed the boat on your boat party?"

"No, because I found a ladder."

I kiss his neck next. "Do you want to know how astronauts have sex?"

I pull the blanket tightly over us to keep us together. I press myself as close to him as possible. "Don't let go or I'll float away."

We make love until we are weightless, two small bodies locked together inside a vast galaxy. We flail against gravity, but we hang on to each other. Above us, six green planets sway in their glass orbs. A gentle susurration rises from the corner, and a shower of plaster falls onto the ground like bits of star and moon dust.

As it turns out, a ladder is exactly what our home needs. Although standing the ladder up can take quite a bit of space, this is well worth having another level. Now we have a single-occupancy loft. This is perfect for getting some time alone. The high altitude offers a peaceful location for clearing your head and seeing things from a different perspective.

Plus, when we are done with it, we can easily fold the ladder up and tuck it away. In its dormant state, the ladder makes a perfect place for laying wet clothes out to dry.

I am slowly filling up the shelves with books. At the library, they sell old books for fifty cents. I go to there to work on job applications, searching the thesaurus for strong, hardworking verbs to add to my resume. Each time I submit an application, I select one book to take home. I like to pick ones with full-page pictures — images of our planet from NASA satellites, diagrams of edible Northwest plants, faded photographs of culinary creations from the seventies.

Carson already has two jobs but he is looking for another, because neither of the jobs is as fulfilling as the right job could be.

Some nights, he asks me what would make me happier.

I try to think of the verbs, but they skip away from me. I am left only with *want*. But *want* is a verb that demands a direct object and I don't know what my direct object is.

Ellen, who I met at the library, says I am good at verbs. She asked me if I could help her update her résumé. She is changing career paths, from nurse to something in marketing. Maurice wants a job where he can lift boxes and not talk to people. Maurice is not good with computers so Ellen and I help him check his email and fill out his applications. Maurice has endless applications to complete. Those for jobs and those for food stamps, utilities discounts, transit cards, healthcare claims.

"I've got everything," I tell Carson.

"You can have more."

Sometimes what I want is less. I want nothing but this bed and a few books, so we can lie down together and look at photographs.

"I just want you to be happy," Carson says.

I do all the things that will show him I am happy. I bake bananas with ham, which is what they ate in the seventies. I swallow a handful of vitamin D each morning with tea. I keep the house clean and the bed made and the bright side on my face. When plaster falls from the ceiling, I sweep the floor and throw the debris away.

Carson and I met at a benefit concert for the men's hockey team, which never really did exist but that didn't stop them trying. They threw the best fundraising parties. The opening band was called Sweet Puck All, and I was sleeping with their drummer. Carson was selling poems for donation, seated at a long table with other poetry students and their personal typewriters. He didn't have a typewriter so he was painting his poems onto squares of stock paper with black India ink. Mine had two words: *beauty* and *fear*.

"What does it mean?" I asked.

"What every poem means," he said.

"Your calligraphy's nice."

"Thanks. Remember to skate without fear."

At some point during the night, I lost the poem on its square paper. After the event we ended up beneath the same awning as the rain tapped its rhythm above us. The drummer had left with a girl he said was his sister. She didn't touch him like a sister. Underneath the awning, Carson offered me gum and a shared cab ride, but I said I was fine walking. He lent me his jacket instead. I returned it to him later that week at the place with the sweet potato pancakes.

That was almost two years ago. When I ask him about the pancakes now, he says he prefers savory breakfast over sweet. Living with another person, you learn that so much of what you thought you knew about them is actually untrue. This is one of the risks of living together that I had not considered.

Carson says that either way, we need to give living together a chance. That is part of evolution. Without evolution, there is only extinction.

Sometimes I look at him and wonder what I would do if he

died. If I died, I know what he would do. He would spend a few weeks or months climbing mountains, and on top of the mountains, he would write poems for me. Eventually, he would become a celebrated poet with a heartbreaking history. This would be its own happy ending. But if Carson died, I would be stranded.

This is unfair, and I am entirely to blame.

Ellen says we all get lost in life sometimes. Every time she switched to a new wing of the hospital, she spent a few days completely lost. For years now, she's wandered from one patient's room to another, convincing herself she could help, and that she cared about helping. The truth was, she'd known the very first day that the hospital wasn't her place, but she couldn't get out because she'd never made her five-year plan.

I ask her how one goes about making a five-year plan.

"You have to start with a vision," she says, "of where you want to be in five years. That's your objective. Then, you decide what you will do during each year to help you meet your objective. Those are your goals. They need to be smart goals. Small, measurable, achievable, and a few other things. You enter them into a spreadsheet."

Ellen has been learning about spreadsheets and plans to use them to track medications, once she is marketing and not administering them. Since she now has her five-year plan, she is making one-year plans, quarterly plans, monthly plans. Sometimes she even plans out our whole afternoon.

"Maurice," she says. "You've got five minutes left, so focus."

She turns to me. "And you. You need to come up with a vision."

I fill a page of my notebook with pen swirls trailing stars.

"If you know a goal is achievable, does that still count as a goal?" I ask Ellen.

"Knowing that something is achievable is very different from achieving it."

This is true, and we think about this quietly.

Maurice throws a pencil at us from the other side of the table. It clatters against the fake wood laminate. "Hey, dimwits. How about a little focus?"

Although Ellen and Maurice started out strangers, they are becoming more and more beautiful. Ellen has a frail face and gray hair. Her curls are tight and vibrant. She has dyed a lock of it bright blue and the neon streak is tucked behind her right ear. Maurice is bulky with a large head that sinks down into his chest. At first he is intimidating, but now I am charmed by his smile, which brings out two deep dimples in the middle of his cheeks. His size has made him shy and sometimes embarrassed, like when we first met at the career fair, and he knocked over one of the posters on display. Now we are his friends, so he is not afraid to throw pencils at us to keep us focused.

I invite Carson to the library to work with us, on one of the afternoons he is not at a job. I immediately regret doing so, but it is too late to take it back.

When he sits with us, the whole dynamic changes. Ellen keeps her lips pursed and her face stern. Maurice is silent and avoids eye contact. I wish that he had not chosen today to wear a dirty T-shirt. It smells like yesterday's sweat.

Carson makes small talk and asks about our interests and daily schedules, but we all know that he is not like the rest of us.

Ellen has added feathers to her hair. Three brown, spotted

feathers dangle from the lock of blue hair along with several earthen beads. I wonder if Carson thinks this is tacky. I wonder if I would appreciate the feathers more if he were not sitting next to me.

Sometimes you see your friends as beautiful because you love them, but no one is really beautiful. It is only loving them that makes them so. Other times you look again and see what the rest of the world must see. Then you are forced to make excuses for them.

I wonder what excuses Carson has made for me. When he tells me I am beautiful, I want to ask for the specifics and the comparison over time. Have my freckles aged? Has my cellulite spread? Have I said anything to expose a lack of knowledge or a simple mind? No one is beautiful always. Sitting next to his friends at pub trivia, at dinner parties, at taprooms, I try to say the right things, or if not that, then at least blend into the background. I feel as embarrassed as Maurice. I forget that Maurice has a lovely and affecting smile.

When Carson suggests we have a housewarming party, with a guessing game as to how many people will fit inside our home, all I can imagine is a crowd of strangers breathing our air, until there is no more left for the two of us. I feel sick in my stomach.

"Why can't we invite Ellen and Maurice?" I say, after he lists some of the people who will come.

"Of course we can invite them," he says. "I just didn't think this was the kind of thing they'd enjoy."

"Everyone enjoys a party," I say, even though I know that Ellen and Maurice would not enjoy such a thing and I don't actually want them to come.

"Okay, then. Let's invite them," he says, and so we do.

For the special occasion of our first party, we string Christmas lights up along our ladder and stand it up in the back corner near the oven and the fridge, not far from the crack where the plaster falls. Carson cleans and folds up our bed, leaning the mattress against the wall. I make a salad from the 1970s, suspending chunks of pineapple in green Jell-O, whipping marshmallows with heavy cream.

Ellen is the first to arrive. For the party, she has added more feathers to her hair. On the right side, they are small and brown and neat, much like the original three. On the left are two big black feathers that look like they have seen rough winds. The white quills are bare at some points. I think maybe she has picked these feathers off the street.

I stick close to her. The two of us with Maurice are like our own little planet. Our magnetic force repels intruders. Everywhere we go, people steer clear, unable to break through our stratosphere.

Someone laughs at the case of beer that Maurice has brought, because of its low quality or association to an unfavorable sub-culture. I try to make him feel better but I don't know how. "I don't think people like my salad, either," I say. Neither he nor Ellen responds.

Carson steps in, picking up the case of beer. "This is just what we need," he says. He places a stack of red plastic cups on the wooden chest and drags it out so it is across from the ladder. Then he places two more cups on the second step of the ladder and conjures three Ping-Pong balls from nowhere.

Ellen sets down her drink and ruffles the feathers inside her hair. "This is my favorite game."

It is so crowded that while four people are playing, the rest of us have to stand packed against the walls. Everyone takes turn playing but Ellen is the only one who is undefeatable, so she stays in the game all night. Carson's friends tell her that she is incredible, that they have never met anyone like her, that they adore everything about her. When it is Maurice's turn, they cheer for him, too. They call him Big Mo and he grants them his lovely smile.

Carson hugs me from behind. "We did a good party, didn't we? Want to do our count?"

I slide away because I don't want him to touch me.

"Aren't you having fun?" he asks.

"Yeah." I try to smile.

"Are you okay?"

"Uh huh."

I feel like he has betrayed me and stolen from me, even though I know that nothing had been mine to steal. I move away from him and congratulate Maurice on a good game. Later, there is talk of going to a bar. Ellen says she knows a place with shuffleboard, and everyone is enamored with the idea of shuffleboard.

"Do you think you'll go out, too?" I ask Maurice.

He shuffles from foot to foot. "I don't know. Maybe."

"I don't know if I'll go out," I say to Carson. "I might just stay here."

"What's wrong?" he asks. His eyes are pleading.

I shrug. "I'd rather be by myself."

"Did I do something?"

I am quiet a moment too long.

"Tell me what's wrong."

"It's nothing. I just like being alone sometimes."

What I have said is too much. As a poet, Carson can be very sensitive. I am tired of caring about this.

"Why do you always choose to be sad," he asks, "when you could choose to be happy?"

"I'm not choosing anything."

He turns away from me, but I still see it when he makes his choice. "I'm going to go out," he says.

"That's fine."

Ellen walks by surrounded by new friends and she does not look in my direction. Maurice tries to tag after her, but he slows down as the rest of the group speeds up.

I think about asking Carson to stay, but I don't. I don't even say good night.

Maurice sticks close to the wall and hugs his elbows over his chest. "Maybe I could help you clean up?"

"No. That's okay," I say. "I'm pretty tired, actually. I might just do it tomorrow."

His back looks lonely when he walks away, but I am not sorry to see him go.

After the noise of the party, the room holds its silence tight. The floor and windowsills are littered with empty cups and bottles, and the space echoes like an abandoned wreck, like the wake of an asteroid. I feel polluted. I dump the trash into a large plastic bag, but the atmosphere is stained by new smells and events. I mop the floor and try to wipe everything away. Mopping makes me tired, but nothing more.

I lie in bed with the lights on, not sure if I will sleep. Our little room seems larger than before, a vast and cold galaxy, and I am shrinking ever smaller. An astronaut unmoored in space never stops falling, uncertain when and if they'll ever tumble back to land. *Can you see me? Can you hear me?* But the signal's gone out and no one's waiting, not here in this great expanse. The air plants glow inside their crystal balls. I count them over and over.

VISITING HOURS

Michelle could not remember the last time she slept through the night. For months now, her eyes would snap open at 4:01 a.m. The glowing digital numbers taunted her from the clock on her nightstand. Sometimes she fell back to sleep but more often, her mind refused rest. Her dreams were strange of late. Places she hadn't visited in years, people she hadn't seen. The scent of someone she once held dear seemed to linger in the air when she woke.

She banished the dreams by scrolling through headlines on her phone. Once that got too dire, she'd get on the exercise bike, make coffee, start in on case reviews. The cat would stir from his perch by the window just long enough to express disapproval before turning a circle in his bed and returning to sleep. She herself would not be able to sleep again until after lunch, when she crashed hard but had to rouse soon after for afternoon briefings.

She could not say for sure when this became her routine, but it was not because of Jason. When he first moved out, she had slept in absolute peace, relishing every inch of that big empty bed, not a single thought for someone else's comfort or emotions or need for temperature regulation.

Her dad would bring up Jason today. He always did. He had book recommendations for Jason, technology questions, the perfect Christmas gift idea. She knew when they broke up that her father would suffer most. Jason was the son he never had, the buddy who took him out to baseball games and expressed interest in all his proffered opinions. (How could you trust someone like that, someone so eager to please?)

It would have been useful to have Jason around, trustworthy or not, as they moved her mother into the care facility at Mountlake Terrace. An extra pair of hands, plus his preternatural ability to cheer up her dad, who looked smaller and sadder than ever. Her mother was in good spirits, at least. She offered Michelle tea and cakes and roast duck, her pleasant smile signifying lack of recognition.

"Ready to meet some new friends?" Michelle asked her. "It's the big day."

Her dad wanted to check all the luggage again, so Michelle took her mom to the bedroom to help her get ready. She brushed out her silver-stranded hair and clasped a string of turquoise beads around her neck.

"You're so pretty, mom."

"You're the pretty one, Wen. Everyone says so."

She was in the past then, mistaking Michelle for a childhood friend. Her mother, the time traveler, twisting history like a loop of silk. Michelle preferred to think of it this way — her mother traversing across decades, wielding a new superpower versus disease.

Her dad was still standing in the living room, forlorn.

"Should we bring the horse painting? Will that make it feel more like home?" He spoke quietly as if to himself.

Many of his conversations were one-sided now, but that was better than nothing. Michelle imagined him puttering from room to room, speaking to air. They couldn't put it off any longer though. Twice now, her mother had wandered off on her own. Once, she got up in the middle of the night to cook and left an empty pot on the burner.

"Why don't we decide about the painting later?" Michelle said. "We have time."

Michelle doubted her mother had any attachment to the horses. At some point the painting had gone onto the wall and they never found the need to hang up another.

The care facility looked even more drab than it did on the tour, window blinds dusty and wheelchair tracks staining the linoleum floor of the lobby. They walked around the gardens first while the staff helped move their things, then shared a bland and very mushy meal in the cafeteria.

Her mother remained unbothered until they returned to her room. Michelle sat with her while her dad completed some paperwork in the office. Her smile slipped away.

She grabbed Michelle's wrist, her grip almost painful.

"What kind of daughter are you?"

"Mom?"

"Are you clever enough for my ghost?"

Michelle made her own voice firm. "I don't believe in ghosts."

In the last few months, her mother had started speaking about her ghost, as if she felt her life fading.

"Ghost will go to you. Ghost always needs somebody." Her eyes glazed over. She continued murmuring softly.

"I'll come visit lots, okay? Mom?" Michelle tried to call her out of her trance.

When her dad returned with the nurse, her mom's expression was blank again, all her different selves shuttered inside.

"Good afternoon, Mrs. Liu." The nurse was full of false cheer. "What a busy day for you. We're so happy you've joined us here."

Michelle cringed at the saccharine tone. She nudged her dad. "Should we go?"

He was reluctant, trying to call her mother's attention to the framed family photos he'd laid out.

Michelle tried again. "If you want to work on the basement today, then we better go."

He followed her out like a reprimanded child. She hadn't meant to hurt his feelings, but she wasn't in the mood to apologize.

———

Her parents' basement. Where to begin?

Her parents' basement was where you stashed away the things you didn't speak out loud, things you would rather forget, things you never wanted to see again.

It was the place you hid the body. When she thought she'd killed her hamster and was too ashamed to tell anyone, she tossed him into a corner of the basement. No one noticed he was missing for a month. She told her parents he ran away. The body was never recovered.

When the first spiders showed up in her parents' basement, they observed the exposed beams and the cracks in the concrete and they saw an opportunity to prosper. Generations upon generations of spiders lived and spawned and died.

When she came out to her parents, she came out from the basement. She'd dripped with sweat and shame as she came clean about the relationship blossoming with her LSAT tutor. In the end, it was for nothing. Her dad claimed to already know, her mother didn't remember, and the tutor moved to New York a month later.

The basement was where you shed your past lives: stacks of LSAT prep books, a Ketchup-stained prom dress, complete

DVD sets of *The OC* and *Veronica Mars* and other worlds you dreamed of inhabiting, padded cotton jackets sewn together by your grandmother for those lonely nights on foreign land, old photographs of people you once loved.

Also: old photographs of people you'd never met, the edges of which were sometimes indented with curious bite marks the size of a small rodent's, perhaps a hamster's.

Half the shit in her parents' basement never belonged to them. People came on tourist visas and left quickly as jobs cropped up in other states. The church her parents attended asked them to host missionaries who brought gifts and Bibles they forgot to pack up when they left. Relatives of family friends passed away, their possessions offered up for use and enjoyment. Her parents could never turn down anything free.

There are things her mother talks about now—long-gone items she's never mentioned, names she's never spoken—unearthed from the basement. Michelle sweeps back the cobwebs and wonders what unutterable things will be unearthed one day from her own mind.

"Probably garbage," her dad said.

"What?"

He held out a dusty cardboard box. "Take a look through it. She labeled it for you. She must have picked things out for you." Then, at her confusion. "You don't have to keep anything you don't want to."

She accepted the box. "I'll take it home."

"Let's call it a day, huh?" he said. "Hungry?"

He made his usual—fried rice with peas, corn, and cubes of ham. Though he'd taken on the cooking duties later in life, this was still the only dish he'd truly mastered.

Michelle found it a bit too salty, but she shoveled a big spoonful into her mouth when the conversation turned naturally to Jason.

"He called to send his best for Mom."

Michelle nodded.

"He had some news of his own to share."

"Mmhmm?"

"You may already know. He's seeing someone new."

Michelle had not known, but she was happy for him. She knew how much it mattered—he'd never learned how to be by himself.

"He plans to propose soon."

Her first instinct was to laugh. She managed to hold it in. "Did he call to ask your permission?"

He made a face like he'd just had reflux. "It's not the first time he's asked, you know."

Michelle looked down guiltily, also hiding a surge of annoyance. Did Jason really have to bring her parents into everything?

"I told him I support him, but also that I thought he was moving too fast."

"Yeah, we only broke up five months ago."

"Four and a half."

"Someone's counting."

"There's something I'd like to say." He cleared his throat.

"It's been a really long day, Dad."

No time for a nap that day. Every cell in her body was suddenly tired.

"You were his first choice. He wanted to marry you. If you say yes now, it might not be too late."

"Dad, don't."

"He'll be good to you, haizi. What more can you want? Some choices, you know, you regret your whole life."

"Not this one. Okay? No regrets for me."

"A good man like him. You won't find another one easily."

"I know you guys got along. I wish you could marry him. I do."

"Everything is a joke to you. After I die, you will be alone. Who will look after you?"

"Don't be dramatic. You're in great health. We should sign you up for pickleball."

"Uncle Lou sprained his ankle and his wrist trying to play that game. His daughter has three kids. They help him carry his groceries, pick up the mail. You don't want to have children?"

"Kids are a lot of work. Don't you know Mom's already given me a ghost? So I've got that to deal with."

He shook his head and took off his glasses, cleaning them on the hem of his shirt. "You have only the one chance to live. Do with it what you see fit."

He didn't have the energy to push more, shoulders slumping. She missed with a pang the heatedness of their old arguments. She wanted him to slam a hand on the table, threaten her with the things he could take away, as if the world were his to give. She longed for the safety of childhood.

———

4:01 and the room was washed in strange light. The screen of her laptop glowed in the darkness. Some kind of alert had turned it back on, maybe.

4:03 and a plane passed overhead, its low rumble cutting through the silence.

4:06. Thudding noises from downstairs or outside. The neighbor? Or the ghost coming to call?

4:10. Her patience ran out. She was awake and there was no point trying to sleep. At the peal of a distant siren, she flipped aside the covers and grabbed her laptop. No new messages or updates. She opened a browser window. What was there to do on the Internet at this hour besides stalk your soon to be engaged ex?

Jason was tasteful as always. No salacious photos. No photos at all. Mr. Emily No-Post. Why couldn't he just lay it out there with some sloppy-drunk party pics or a coy close-up of their fingers entwined? Why couldn't he just be a normal asshole? She could have been happy with a normal asshole. Someone who didn't demand too much, didn't make her fall short.

She jumped over to a few of the average, everyday assholes she had dated before, found photo evidence of their normal happy lives, remembered why she could not have chosen them. She went to the outliers instead, the ones where she never really stood a chance. The violinist had become a mother recently. The LSAT tutor was in the process of transitioning.

5:20 suddenly, and she still had yet to search for the most significant ex. Perhaps because she had spent the night dreaming of her.

They met during Michelle's first year in Beijing. Caryn was a few years older, wrapping up her PhD in gender studies in California. As part of Caryn's dissertation, she had returned to China to interview women seeking divorces. She carried a camera with her almost always, stopping during their excursions through the city to ask to photograph or film someone. The woman steaming buns by the subway station. The man who often played cards by himself at the bar they frequented. Sometimes, she'd film their slow, lazy mornings. There was footage of Michelle getting dressed and then being pulled back into bed, getting undressed.

Later, after they broke up and Michelle returned to the U.S., Caryn started writing as well. One of her pieces went viral in an online journal they'd both enjoyed. A queer love story—from the lightning strike of attraction through the slow baring of self, followed by abrupt separation, being ghosted, abandoned, cut off from the one you had dared to share yourself with.

Michelle burned in recognition of herself: *doe-eyed virgin . . . terrified of her own truths . . . beyond the firewall—her ice shelf of silence.* She read the comments obsessively. Almost nobody took her side.

Their last conversation was an argument.

"You should have asked," Michelle said. "Also, you lied. I didn't ghost you. You said you didn't want to be in touch."

"I tried contacting you later."

"My mother just got diagnosed. I was busy."

"If you hadn't blocked me," Caryn said, "I would have let you know."

"If you'd wanted to, you would have found a way. A phone call, for instance."

Caryn's defense, finally, was that she didn't know the piece would get so many readers or that it would be accepted at all.

"Don't ever write about me again," Michelle said before hanging up.

That essay was one of the few artifacts of their relationship. Having met away from home, they never orbited into each other's communities. There were photos, of course, but saved on some old hard drive Michelle had lost track of.

Caryn went on to write about far more interesting things than their relationship: factory workers, labor movements, gender equality. Long ago, Michelle had harbored the fantasy of Caryn returning to the U.S., their relationship rekindling without the barrier of geography. She couldn't remember anymore why they had fought so bitterly. It was obvious to her now, the pull of responsibility on them both. It seemed now they had only wanted from each other a little more compassion. Had it been so impossible to grant this at the time, or in the many years after?

The last updates on Caryn's website were from half a year ago. She'd closed her accounts on most other platforms.

Her most recent project: a series of photo essays called *Exemplary Women*. Michelle remembered Caryn telling her about a Ming dynasty tome, collected by an empress to instruct women on how to behave. In those stories, women were virtuous and brave and fiercely devoted. They plunged to their deaths or drowned or fell upon angry swords to save their husbands, children, country. In Caryn's series, she paired stark, black and white photographs of individual women with their stories of sacrifice and survival under patriarchy.

Her website included a form submission for getting in touch. Michelle hovered the mouse over the empty boxes. The cursor blinked impatiently.

I hope you're well, she typed. *Be safe. Be happy. I miss you.*

To borrow Caryn's logic, she sent it only because she didn't think it would go through. But that didn't mean she wasn't inviting trouble.

———

The staff was meant to call every day the first week of her mother's stay to provide regular updates. Michelle had expected them to reach out to her dad and panicked when she saw the string of missed calls from a number she did not know.

The voicemails were garbled. Static in the first one and a loud rustling in the second. A voice seemed to emerge in the third, but it was so scratchy it sounded like forks being dragged across the throat. The rustling fell away in the last message, but the vowels stretched long into a moan, building in volume until it became almost too painful to listen to.

Michelle deleted it and dialed her dad. "Everything okay?"

He was already on site. There were no limits to visiting hours at the facility, though they asked that families be respectful toward the needs of all residents.

"Their hot water dispenser is broken," he said. "We need to get an electric kettle."

As they got older, her parents cleaved even harder to the idea that the root of all ailments was drinking cold water.

"I'll pick one up after work and bring it by," Michelle said.

It was hard to focus, though, after a morning spent stalking Caryn, reading her work, studying her recent photos. In one shot, her hair was a pale, frosty blue. In another, it was back to black but cropped short. While her writing was easy to find, there was very little information about her personal life, Michelle realized with frustration.

She tried to distract herself with the box from the basement. She recognized the porcelain tea set with the painted cat she had admired during childhood afternoons at Grand Auntie Du's, while her mother cleaned and cared for the church elder. She found an album of black and white photos — Grand Auntie Du's people. Having survived them all, the old woman had left her possessions to Michelle's mom, who promptly packed it away into the basement.

At the bottom of the box, she found three unopened letters, Caryn's handwriting on the outside of the crinkled envelopes. Fuck. Michelle remembered the anger that pulled taut inside her when she'd tossed these letters into the wastebin. In the end, she'd fished them back out, tucked them into a desk drawer. Somehow, they'd found her in the basement.

She set the letters down. Whatever they contained, it was still too much.

She opened the lacquered jewelry box instead, making herself admire the intricate carving of birds and bamboo on the lid. Nothing in there with the power to hurt. She'd expected to find nothing inside at all, but there was a pair of gold earrings and a black silk sachet. She swiped a finger through the sachet, surprised again to brush against something small and prickly.

"What the hell is this?" She showed her dad the wisps of hair, the slivers of fingernail, delivering the sachet along with the electric kettle.

"Throw it away," he said.

Her mother, though, grabbed hold of the sachet and clutched it to her chest. "So little remains. Just dust in the end. It's so heavy, though. The soul is so heavy."

Michelle looked to her dad, who shrugged helplessly. They never knew what to do when her mother revealed a new personality.

She grabbed Michelle's hands. "She is looking for you," she said. "She won't rest until she finds you. Let her in. Do it for yourself."

"Who?" Michelle asked, as a cold shudder rippled down her spine. Not Caryn. It couldn't be Caryn. She was not superstitious enough for this shit. "Mom. Want to go on a walk? How about we go see the gardens again? Won't the sunshine be nice?"

She took the sachet back and stuffed it into her pocket. Whatever it was, she didn't want it disturbing her mother.

Outside, the clouds were accumulating. Since their walk the day before, a windstorm had stripped the branches nearly bare. The last golden leaves shivered in the breeze. Michelle remembered the Tang dynasty poem Caryn taught her. At dawn, the writer hears birdsong all around, sweet melodies after a night of thrashing wind and rain. Upon waking, who could say how many petals lay scattered on the ground?

The wind was roaring again when Michelle woke the next day. 4:01 and no birdsong. The empty hour. Another thud outside, like the night before but louder. The wind blowing something over? She went down to investigate, using her phone as a flashlight. The cat was already there, hissing at the door. He sat stiffly at the foot of the stairs, eyes glittering.

"What you looking at, Spark?" Michelle asked.

The phone juddered in her hand, its screen lighting up.

She didn't recognize the number, but she saw the text.

It's me. Got your message. I'm in Seattle! But only here for a few more hours. I tried calling but it wouldn't go through. Are you around? I'm outside.

Her heart hammered against her chest in the same rhythm as the knock on the door.

It must be some kind of trick. She knew this, yet she still opened the door, and there was Caryn standing in the rain.

"Hi," she said. "Can I come in?"

Her smile was the same as before. It elicited the same leap of joy in Michelle's stomach, a kick of nervous energy.

"Looks cold out there." That was all she could think to say as she opened the door wide.

The cat yowled as Caryn entered. He hissed once then ran away, gray tail swishing.

"I have to leave before it gets light," Caryn explained. "It was a long shot, but I thought I'd try. I wouldn't be able to let it go if I didn't try."

"How did you get my address?"

Caryn shrugged. "I'm a journalist. I know how to track people down."

Michelle filled the kettle with water. "Tea?"

Caryn nodded gratefully.

Michelle busied herself in the kitchen, if only so she could catch a breath, give herself a minute. Her hands shook as she tried to break off a few pieces of dried Pu-erh.

"What brings you out here?" she asked. "Are you back, like, working?"

What she meant: Are you here a lot?

Caryn shook her head. "It's a quick trip. I'm just working on a story, trying to wrap it up. God, that smells good."

She closed her eyes as she breathed deeply over the tea. Michelle took the opportunity to study her face, charting the changes, anchoring herself in the familiar constellation of freckles on her left cheek. Old memories surfaced. They tingled on her skin, goosebumps rising. Caryn still looked the same. She looked like herself, not those other versions of her on the Internet. Her hair was tied back in a loose, messy bun, reddish-brown highlights shining through. Her eyes, heavily lidded, were curious but cautious. This was her guarded, professional mode, when she kept all her boundless energy restrained until she knew what questions to ask, where to prod.

"You look great," Michelle said. "You look like someone I know." Her cheeks burned, embarrassed after hearing the thought out loud. How could she still know this person, really, after all these years, nearly a decade. "It's been a long time, I mean."

Caryn took it well. She moved closer and brushed a lock of Michelle's hair back behind her ear. "I still know you a little."

Maybe a decade was only an inch of time, in the long run. Maybe time only worked as a unit of measure if each day repeated itself in the same way. Did you hurtle through time or did time slip away? If she kissed her right now, would time stop? For how long?

"I can't believe you're here," Michelle whispered.

"I didn't want to go without seeing you. I was so glad to hear from you."

She reached for Michelle. Time did not stop for a kiss. It compounded instead—all the kisses they had shared before reverberating in a moment. Time folded in on itself, entangled past with present, compressed and collapsed onto them until they broke away, gasping.

Caryn stepped back and then toward the living room. "I love your place," she said. "It's so adult. It's all yours?"

"Yeah. I've had roommates and such, but the place is mine." Boyfriend, roommate? Did she have to elaborate?

"And you have a cat?"

The cat was making himself known again, baring his incisors and yowling at Caryn.

"Get a grip, Spark." Michelle shooed him away. "He's usually less neurotic."

"Look at you," Caryn said. "Homeowner. Pet owner. The definition of thriving, right?"

"Missing a car, missing a man. Missing 2.5 kids and a white picket fence," Michelle smiled, remembering how they had taunted the American dream. "Look at you, though, living your own dream. I read some of your stuff. I love the new project, the women's stories. They're, like, private victories, but so powerful shared with others."

Suddenly she was shy again, and so inarticulate.

"Thank you," Caryn said. "I didn't want them to be forgotten. So many things get buried. I just wanted to make a few people look."

"That's what you used to say, too, when I got sick of you pulling out your camera. Your work is amazing."

Caryn shrugged. "Who's paying attention, really? We're all forgotten in the end."

Michelle reached for her again, grasped for something of the past, some way to go back. "I tried to forget you. I never really could."

That soul-sucking smile. "That's because we were incomplete. Sometimes our lives stutter, and we cannot just be. We try again and again to repeat or to remember something. We only forget the things that were perfect. Perfect is boring." She shrugged. "I read that in a book once. It made me think of you."

"That's me. A model of imperfection."

"I wanted to forget you, too," Caryn said. "It's much easier, isn't it? To forget?"

Michelle thought of all the things her mother had needed to

forget in order to build her life an ocean away from the world she knew. Friends she left behind. Friends who went missing, left the world without a trace. Forgetting was a means of survival. Forgetting was a clinical diagnosis. The things she'd put behind her now chased her down the winding corridors of memory.

"How is your mom doing?" Caryn asked, as if reading her mind.

"She has some good days."

"I wish I could have a second chance. I could have been so much more supportive. I should have been better."

Apologies made Michelle uncomfortable. She squirmed under the emotional weight. "You did what you had to do. I wasn't the most generous at the time. I didn't mean for things to end the way they did, though. I didn't want that."

Caryn leaned closer, her breath cool against Michelle's cheek. "If we'd ended better, then maybe you would forget me."

"I haven't managed to yet."

Michelle's turn to initiate. The kiss sent a chill down her spine. Recognition was so clear. There you are—I've searched for you my whole life. Don't let me lose you again. She searched for the right things to say, something that would make Caryn stay.

"I'm glad you wrote about me. Nothing exemplary or brave in there, but it's nice to know our story was written down."

"You hated it." Caryn grinned, teasing. "Makes sense. I never let you tell your side."

"Maybe it's time to revise it, write a new ending?"

Caryn shook her head. "We can't live in the past. The past is a trap. Too many memories spoil the present, and the present is all we really ever have."

The present swelled with Caryn, cracked open to make space

for her. She took up every inch and more, beyond measure. Michelle gave in to the dizzying afterglow of her touch. She let go of the questions—*where have you been? where are you going?* The only thing that needed to be said: *I'm so happy it's you.* Their bodies expressed this so completely, words were not necessary.

Caryn had things to tell her, though, moving into her brisk, animated reporter mode. Michelle tried to listen, feeling drunk in her presence. Images of Caryn's life flashed through Michelle's mind—hiding flash drives loaded with her footage, watching activists get arrested in the middle of the night, running from police. Michelle had missed so much. She struggled to keep up.

"I want you to know," Caryn said. "I want to be known by you."

Michelle could not track then versus now. Time unraveled. The light changed. The sun was rising. One bright ray arched through the window, briefly blinding her. Suddenly it was quiet. She blinked the room back into view, but Caryn was missing.

On the windowsill, the black silk sachet sat waiting.

It was heavier than before. Michelle reached in and pulled out a lock of black hair, lightly streaked with copper. She looped the hair twice around her middle and index fingers. It smelled of wild sage, burning grasses.

———

Weeks passed before her mother mentioned the ghost again. Michelle was sitting with her in the library of the care facility, looking out the window at the bare branches. They were quiet for a long time before her mother spoke.

"She will not bother you again."

Michelle looked up from her phone. "Who?"

She was reading reportage from China. A number of lawyers had recently been arrested. A beloved actress was missing, no posts online for the past three months. Family members of a young journalist were holding vigil outside a police station.

After that night, Michelle tried to get in touch with Caryn again, returning the text message. *Wrong number, sweetheart,* her query returned.

"You choose how much of the past you hold onto," her mother said. "I won't ask you to carry anything for me. Neither will she."

Michelle closed her eyes and took a breath. Suppose she could suspend reality. If not now, then when?

Her mother studied her kindly, eyes fully aware.

"Did you send her to me?" Michelle asked. "Did you help her find me?"

"Tell me her name, the one you loved."

Michelle did so.

Her mother took her hand. "I won't forget it."

Sorrow plunged through her like a stone sinking into water. The water was so deep, it would never touch bottom. She'd thought she knew what the ocean was, but its vastness was incomprehensible. All around her, the world was shifting and changing. She could not guess how or what the world would be once she emerged.

"It's okay," her mother said, patting her shoulder. "You'll be fine."

Michelle leaned close and tucked her cheek against her mother's shoulder, those bones so much frailer now. She hadn't sat like this since she was a child, but her mother's hand stroked her back, solid and warm and full of reassurance, for at least one moment more.

JOY COMES IN
THE MORNING

I went over to Rosalind's house because the Sunday Sisters had gathered to pray for me. I told them I didn't believe in God but attended services with my mother because it pleased her, and I wanted to give her that, so they prayed for God to lift the veil from my eyes and soften my heart, that I might accept his love, which made me fidget in the wicker rocking chair—the only single-occupant seat in the room—but that was not the most uncomfortable part.

The most uncomfortable part was the photo on the mantelpiece, blown up and stretched onto canvas so I could study in magnified detail the man I used to date. Pete, at possibly his peak of handsome and happy, arms wrapped around Rosalind and all that airbrushed bliss. The last time I'd slept with him was over ten years ago, so it made sense that I wasn't sure if I could recognize him, which is not to say that perhaps it wasn't him because it definitely was, but that he was maybe not the same person I once knew.

I might have known that Rosalind's husband was Pete, had I been paying better attention. My mother didn't know our romantic history, but she'd probably mentioned the wedding to me, among a long list of updates about other people I no longer cared to keep up with.

The woman with the cat eye glasses began to pray for my mother, who was at home, dying, but the woman didn't seem to know this as she kept saying things like "feel better" and "back on her feet," like the problem was a sprained ankle. In fact, my mother had been on her feet just fine that morning during the worship service. Confusing, no doubt. In the silence that followed, Rosalind opened her eyes to give me an apologetic smile. The other five women kept their heads bowed over clasped hands.

Wrapping up, Rosalind thanked God for his blessings and clarified my mother's condition without causing embarrassment or breaking confidence. She was very eloquent and also very tall. Stately. I wondered where she had gone to high school. Not around here.

After she finished, collective relief rustled through the circle and six sets of eyes turned my way.

"Thank you," I said, taking a careful sip of tea. "That was very kind of you all."

"I hope you feel refreshed," the redhead said.

I nodded, afraid to say the wrong thing and disrupt the post-prayer solemnity.

Rosalind spread her Bible open on her lap. She was a quietly stunning woman, honey blonde hair cut in a neat shoulder-length bob, high cheekbones, and a thin patrician nose—if ever there was a nose that could be described that way. A certain maturity missing in the photograph added to her beauty, or perhaps it was our setting that lent her an air of sorrow. She bent her head forward as she read, the fire casting a warm halo around her. The shadows on her face shifted with her lips as she read to us from the Book of Luke.

A man held his shriveled arm out to Jesus and he was healed. To the women, this meant we had to stop averting our eyes from the broken. God's power was greatest when it was most transformative. Each of us carried our own shriveled arms in need of holy transformation.

I moved in my seat, the rocking chair creaking as it propelled me forward.

"Did you have something to share, Laura?" Rosalind asked.

I shook my head. "It was the chair."

Their smiles wavered but held.

"Could I use your bathroom?" I clutched my purse like I had something important to do.

Rosalind pointed the way. I didn't actually need the bathroom, but I flushed and washed my hands and dried them on the mint green towels. The mirror reflected a framed picture of a mountain lion prowling on the wall behind me. Pete's contribution, probably. It had no place against the coral wallpaper, opposite the arrangement of candles and potpourri and little pastel soaps. A box of matches sat on top of the toilet, next to the burned ones in a little glass jar. It was much too clean to be the bathroom they regularly used but I looked behind the mirror anyway. Bottles of aspirin and ibuprofen, Band-Aids, hydrogen peroxide, a tube of lotion advertising all-natural beeswax. Nothing in their house looked natural.

The women were still talking when I returned. I motioned to Rosalind that I was stepping outside. It didn't feel right to smoke on their lawn, so I walked to my car and sat against the hood. The sun was down, the sky still dappled with gentle swathes of amethyst clouds that softened the bite of the October chill. They lived on one of the new streets. Sprawling multistory houses, combed lawns, well-placed topiaries. And in the distance, the cornfields, the woods, the old mill.

There had been a time, after the paper mill explosion, when everyone was pushing to move away and those who found jobs or came into money did so. I was fourteen and Pete seventeen. Even then, I knew I had to get out. Later, drawn by the strange beauty of the sunsets or whatever else, a new group of residents flooded in, rebuilding the town so it was almost an attraction. It offered some odd glamour missing from the cities or suburbs, plus premium fishing and hunting. So even though I had made it out of this place, at least for a while, there was no pride to be felt in my escape. I had gotten nowhere better. The town, however, was featured in local magazines.

A truck pulled up. It had to be Pete. I dropped the cigarette and stamped it out.

"Laura? Is that you?" He toed the edge of the lawn, studying me but unwilling to step closer. "What are you doing here?"

His height surprised me, though it shouldn't have. He'd finished growing last I saw him. Perhaps the extra weight made him seem bigger overall. Padded. His straw-blond hair stuck down against his scalp, thinned out and receding. He wore a blue polo and loose jeans smudged with dirt. A tool belt was looped over his arm, indenting the brown paper bag he hugged to his chest.

I raised my hand in a wave. "Hi. How are you?"

"Your mom said you were moving back. Roz invite you to prayer group?"

"Yeah. She's real nice." The way I said it sounded strange, like I was defending her when she hadn't been attacked.

"You weren't really the praying type."

"You're right. That's why I'm out here."

I remembered how appraising his eyes were: icy blue and quick to detect any small deceit. Calculating. He grew familiar again, but then I knew even less what to say.

"Nice house. I like the mountain lion."

"The what?"

"In the bathroom."

"Oh. Right." He shifted the bag to the other arm. "So what are you doing? Where are you working?"

"I'm a teacher."

He raised an eyebrow.

"Yeah. I teach art. But our budget got cut so I'm looking for a new school. Know of any?"

"Any schools?"

"No. It's good. I have time to take care of my mom now."

He shook his head. "She's a great woman, your mom. Got a bad hand. I always liked her. Roz and I have been praying for her."

I wanted to ask him how he'd met Rosalind, what made him fall in love and if it had stuck, how they decided what to hang on their walls, if she knew about his DUI, if he ever finished his degree, if the back of the neck was still his favorite place to kiss.

Instead, I asked, "And when did you become the praying type?"

"A.A. Met Roz's brother there." He held that even gaze.

"Cool. Sounds like a blast."

"You married?"

"No. But I was engaged for three months once."

I'd meant it as a joke. He didn't smile.

He looked down at my feet. "You still smoking?"

I shrugged, pushing the flattened stub away with my heel like I could brush it under my car. It stayed next to my Keds. "I'm cutting down. I don't smoke in front of my mom or anything."

I thought of that night when I was babysitting at the Clifford's, my first year of high school. Pete came over after the kids went to sleep and found a pack of Camels wedged between the couch cushions. He taught me how to smoke and exhale over my shoulder, how to shape smoke rings with my lips. After, we snuck back upstairs to rinse with Listerine, both pretending we still had dads at home waiting to interrogate us.

"You want to go back?" he asked.

"What?"

"Inside the house."

I followed him across the lawn to the lighted steps, watching the swing of his hips and the soft love handles bunching above his jeans. I wondered how the years had built up on me, how much of me he still recognized, how much I had stayed the same.

"Nice seeing you." He held open the door for me.

"Aren't you going to stay?" I asked, as if he were the one entering my home, but he was already walking away, toward the kitchen.

The women were still gathered around the fireplace, laughing now with their Bibles shut. Platters of deviled eggs, fruit, and candied pecans sat on the coffee table.

"I'm so glad you're back." Rosalind reached for me. "Give us a chance, please. We really do try."

They welcomed me into their circle, but I knew I wouldn't sit there long. I would listen to them talk about their kids and their husbands, the latest nutrition fads and the new one-pot recipe. I would smile and nod and eat deviled eggs. We would say good night, and they would return to their brightly lit houses, to husbands who kept the bed warm and children who were always polite, and I would go back to my mother, the house dark except for the light of the television, a pile of my boxes in the guest bedroom that I didn't know whether or not to unpack. I would sit down next to my mother who was waiting and ready to die because it was God's will that she be with Cal again. I would bring her blankets and hot tea, comfort her with tiny lies, guess the answers on whatever game show she was watching, because that was the only thing I could think to do, because for those brief moments, there was something like certainty. For once, I was doing something right.

I saw Pete and Rosalind three days later while picking up medicine at the Walgreens in the strip of stores with the Dairy Queen and Al's Hotdogs. Al's had since become Thai Aroma, which then shut down not long into the pandemic. The darkened windows still bore a "for lease" sign with a phone number in red font.

When I got back to the car and put the key into the ignition, I looked up and there they were. Rosalind laughed at something Pete said. He toted a take-out box of pizza. She grabbed his free hand, or maybe he grabbed hers, because that was something he did now, with her. When they pulled away in Rosalind's silver Ford Explorer, I followed.

It was dark already. I stayed one car behind them. I didn't plan it, but when they turned into a gas station, I turned, too. I parked behind a garbage bin and watched as Pete filled the tank. Rosalind stayed in the driver's seat, looking at her phone.

She worked as a legal secretary and dressed fancy: black slacks and pearl earrings. My mother had said that Pete worked for Rosalind's father, who owned an HVAC company. He wore jeans and a gray fleece.

I followed them all the way till the last turn onto their street.

"What took you so long?" my mother asked when I got back.

"Did they have my prescriptions?"

She retied the dull lavender bathrobe. She wore it constantly. "There was a line."

It was a bad lie but she didn't question it, taking the bag and studying the labels on the bottles. "I'll sleep like a log tonight. Tell me if these things make me snore. Cal always told me what made me snore. Red wine but not white. Chocolate. Claritin. Italian food."

The doctors said they couldn't operate, but they could shrink the tumor with chemo and radiation. Even then, the prognosis promised little. When she first had symptoms, the hospitals and clinics were flooded with Covid cases. Since her tests were negative, she thought it best to stay away. She learned to ignore her cough, her occasional windedness. The doctors made a treatment plan, but having been widowed twice, my mother said she didn't mind the dying part. She just didn't want to die shrunken and bald. Besides, Cal had brought her to the Lord, and both of them were waiting. Without treatment the doctors said nine months—the same amount of time it took to get born. She didn't look like anyone who was dying.

"Any word back from the agency?" she asked.

"Nothing this week but data entry and accounting."

"Accounting. That's something you can learn. You were always good at math. People need accountants these days." Inflation was going up. Recessions were always around the corner. The accountant shortage—that was the problem.

"I already have a career, Mom." I pulled out dishes and silverware.

"There's always time for a change." Her cheerfulness was grating.

"I like my career."

Even though school enrollments were down. Even though no school ever hired more than one art teacher, if any.

"I know, honey." She raised an arm to hug my shoulders. I could feel her frailness through the reassurance of the embrace. "I'm sure you're a good teacher. Maybe you could teach math."

"Sure." I ripped open a bag of salad mix.

"I want you to stay busy while you're here, you know. Find things to do. You shouldn't set aside your whole life just for me. I don't need that." To prove her point, she set a heaping casserole dish onto the trivet. "Chicken and green beans. Grandma's recipe. You know this one, right?"

"Yeah, I think I got that one down." Mostly, it hinged on the canned soup.

"Well, I'm sure you've got your own recipes now."

She took my hand to say grace, thanking the Lord for his bounty on my behalf. She peered at me a moment longer after she let go, her reading glasses resting on the bridge of her nose. The frames matched her purplish red hair. Gray tendrils escaped the loose bun and curled out around the sharp angles of her face.

"God's got a purpose for you, Laura," she said. "Don't you worry. We're not all meant to be artists, but he'll use you like he uses all of us. To God be the glory."

She served a spoonful of casserole onto my plate and then her own. "After I'm gone, you can sell the house. Do something smart with the money. Don't blow it on a vacation. Find something good and invest in it."

That sounded more like my practical mother. Growing up, we had always attended church, but primarily for the social functions. Luncheons and dinners and free Sunday-morning babysitting. My mother never bought into the passion of it, never prayed with much faith or fervency until she met Cal. Through Cal, she found a second life, a redeemed life. She tried to bring me into it too, but I couldn't bring myself to believe, not in God nor in his ability to remake her in his image.

After cleaning up, I stepped outside to call Matthew, who had kept his job as band director back in Madison. We'd become friends over lunchtime smoke breaks and started dating mostly out of boredom. The relationship was never more than luke-warm, but it was also comfortable and convenient. I had one last Lucky Strike from the pack he'd gifted me the day I left, and I was used to the background noise of his sighs and grievances while I smoked.

"Wouldn't you want to travel or do something?" I asked him. "Should I take her on a vacation?"

"Hard enough to travel when you're healthy, let alone when you're sick. I had food poisoning once, on my way back from Bulgaria. Disaster."

Matthew had achieved a spot of fame (his words) when he was younger. He'd traveled across the world playing with bands and symphonies. This helped with job security now but decreased the possibility of job satisfaction. "Another school year," he said. "Every day I think a little longer about shoving a drumstick down my throat."

He had the usual gamut of complaints. Incompetent admin-istrator, spoiled teenagers, overwrought parents. Now that I'd been expunged from that world, I craved its familiar miseries.

"You're lucky, you know," he said. "You got out. You can make a fresh start of it. Sometimes I wonder if what I need is a good kick to the curb."

"You can always quit."

Another sigh. "Don't have it in me. My ashtray attests."

We said good night with no promises to talk again soon. Before I could get back inside, my phone buzzed. I put it to my ear without checking the screen. "Forgot something?"

"I saw you. What are you trying to pull?"

His voice made me freeze. "Pete? Is something wrong?"

An angry pause. "You tell me."

"How did you get my number?" Then I remembered writing it out on a scrap of yellow paper for Rosalind. I pictured her sticking it on the fridge or setting it on their granite counters.

He sucked in his breath. "I thought you put it there. With the mail."

"I didn't."

"Did you follow us?"

I thought about how to explain. "I don't have a lot of places to go."

"Do you need somewhere to go?"

"I don't know. I just—" I looked back toward the house, the brass cherub raising its trumpet over the door knocker. "I just feel a little stuck here."

"I'm not your friend, you know."

"I know you're not."

And then he hung up.

I had almost been an artist. I had come very close. Kind of close.

After undergrad in Wisconsin, I won a place in a somewhat competitive fellowship in New York. Two years of mentorship by six respectable teaching artists. Shared studio space and access to materials, galleries, people. My own spot of fame. I left Madison for Manhattan, prompting Pete to propose. He'd followed me to Wisconsin, found a job repairing bikes and was looking for a way to follow me to New York. For three months, I said yes; then I said no after one of the professors invited me back to his loft and his bed.

I had been warned about the professor, but he was so charming and educational. He introduced me to Scotch, Fellini, escargot. He was well connected. I was thrilled that he had chosen me, the short frumpy one from the flyover state. He seemed to love my plainness, praising my unpretentious features, my domestic face. He would hook a stray brown curl behind my ear and study my face like he was trying to figure out how to paint it—a plain landscape with nothing spectacular. My *ontbijtes*, he called me. A little bite of breakfast with an aftertaste of guilt. I wish I had been more disgusted.

I was naïve and secretly I hoped this would allow me to out-run Pete, who drank too much and tied me to a town that seemed hopeless, an empty mill with too many ghosts. I hadn't realized how much I wanted to get away until I found an exit. But I forgot Pete too easily and perhaps that was my wrong.

The relationship with the professor soured the second year, when a batch of new students arrived, among them a willowy blonde who wore only black, down to the three onyx gemstones studding the corner of her lower lip. There was also the older nude model, but he'd always had her on the side. I stayed with him, still taking his word that he would display my work next to his, that everyone would remember who I was—if I chose a better last name. I thought about asking if I could replace Brown with his name but never had the nerve, though he continued to assure me that I had the most domestic face. When the exhibition approached, he picked Sophie's work instead. How well she would look next to the paintings, so sharp and severe.

Before the opening, I broke into his studio. I found a can of red acrylic and a can of black. I spilled them over the delicate contours of his oils—his contorted nudes and detailed disembodiments. Hands, feet, torsos, streaked in red and black. Standing in front of an abstracted grid of eyes, nose, and lips—which of these features lifted from my face?—I felt fury drip, then gush out of me. Rivers of paint, the fumes heady and pure. Had I ever felt such power before or since, I don't recollect. A few years ago, when I saw his name on the shortlist for a prestigious award, those same trickles of rage returned to me, but I could make no use of it. There was nothing for me to destroy.

He knew at once that I was the culprit. I didn't deny it. I suggested new titles for the exhibit, something like "Retribution in Red." He was not amused. Belonging to the traditional school, he did not believe in the value of spontaneous creation. Later he did give my name to agents and curators, but only to warn them that I was unstable and volatile, a danger to fine art.

I moved back to Madison and got a teaching certificate. Pete had gone back home by then, and I didn't look for him. My mother thought I'd left New York because I grew sick of big city expenses, because I was learning to be pragmatic. She thought Pete had once been a necessary friend with whom I shared my grief, but ultimately, someone I learned to move on from.

She did not know that he had once, in a drunken rage, thrown a vase at me, and then, after watching it shatter by my feet, gotten down on his knees over the limp daffodils and broken glass. She did not know that I had once sat with my back against a door, feeling the vibration his fists made along the wood, until he, too, gave up, and we sat with the door between us until the night turned to dawn and he left to board the plane that would take him out of my life. She did not know that I had willed this to happen, imagining it essential for my life to unfold in an acceptable way.

In the end, what did these things matter? Mine is an old and tedious tale, yet I still want to make it known.

The Sunday Sisters smiled at me less the next prayer meeting. I was no longer new—and this week was not about sinners, it was about saints. Rosalind's college girlfriend, Amalie, was visiting. She had an exotic name and had traveled to exotic places. Raised in South Africa by missionary parents, she now served alongside her husband in Kenya, returning to the U.S. to see to the birth of their third child. The pregnancy was high risk. Gestational diabetes. For this, as for all their missions, they needed prayer and the grace of the Lord.

That was Amalie's refrain. By the grace of the Lord, they had gotten pregnant. By the grace of the Lord, they had gotten to the train station in time. By the grace of the Lord, the plane landed as it was scheduled to land.

As the other women clamored around her, Amalie stroked her belly as she extolled the virtues of having a servant heart and eating a gluten-free diet.

During the break, when the bathroom was occupied, Rosalind gave me permission to wander their house. "Go upstairs. Second door on the right. Amalie loves hogging the bathroom, even when she's not pregnant."

The upstairs bathroom had a Jacuzzi and two sinks. Around one of them, an assortment of lotions and face creams in small glass cylinders. Next to the other, Pete's Philips razor and Old Spice deodorant. Matching electric toothbrushes stood next to their respective sinks. I wanted to turn one of them around, make it face the other way, but they would have noticed, almost certainly.

A second door opened into their bedroom. Finally, some of the mess of their real lives. Pete's clothes were draped over an armchair in the corner. I picked up a navy sweater and folded it, in the neat way that department stores did it, and, I was sure, the way Rosalind did it. On top of the dresser were pearl earrings Rosalind had recently worn and removed, a crumpled receipt, a watch with a thick leather strap — Pete's. The closet smelled like Rosalind, a light floral scent. Inside was all cashmere and silk, so soft and clean, the perfect place to hide.

I found her side of the bed with the help of the leather-bound Bible on the nightstand. I waited until I could no longer resist before I pulled open the drawer. I wanted to know the shape and size of her vibrator, the brand of lube they used. Instead, I found syringes. A whole case, each individually wrapped. Next to it, stacks of alcohol wipes and gauze pads. A few glass vials of medication. Gonal-F. Menopur. A prescription for Zoloft.

Suddenly exhausted, I sat on the bed and lay down across the faint impression her body had left on the duvet. I pressed my cheek against her pillow and counted to ten. Then I took three deep breaths, inhaling all that one leaves behind on a pillow — tears, saliva, strands of hair and sloughed skin cells.

I felt him there before I opened my eyes. He stood watching me from the doorway.

"I'm just really tired," I said.

The tears didn't come until I saw his. I couldn't say why they came, for either of us. He sniffed and pinched the space between his brows to feign a headache, but I knew from the long pause that he was only trying to hide his face.

"We have a guest bedroom," he said. "You can lie down there if you'd like."

"No." I sat up. "I should just go."

I hadn't remembered to shut the drawer. My wrist banged against it as I got up. It continued to throb as I ran down the stairs and out the door.

Pete was not my friend, but after the first big snow, he showed up at our door with a shovel and a basket of muffins. Blueberry.

"Roz made them. She wanted me to take care of your driveway."

"That's so thoughtful of her."

"She says she'd love to see you again, at the next sisters' meeting or wherever."

I had skipped the last two, bowing out on account of my mother. The cold, dry air was hard on her. She had an oxygen tank now.

"Can I get you some coffee?"

He probably would have refused, except my mother came over and called him in.

"Pete," she said. "You're just the person I need. I've been meaning to call you. It's that furnace again."

I followed him down to the basement, thinking I could be of use. Pete switched off a breaker. I shined a weak flashlight on the furnace. He got on his knees and removed a metal panel to examine the nest of wires and levers.

"Ignition seems to be in good shape. It's been making noises?"

"I don't know. I haven't really noticed."

He gave me a look, like I had tricked him into coming down here. To do what? I shrugged at him. He rummaged some more, then said, "I need room to get up."

I moved too quickly, stepping on his fingers. I apologized after he stood and dusted off his jeans.

"Forget it. It's not the worst you've done to me."

"I'm sorry about that, too."

"I probably did worse by you, but here we are." He held up an accordion screen clotted with dust. "Look. This is the filter. This needs to be changed every three months. I'd say this one's been going on two years."

"Cal used to do that, I guess."

"I can grab one for you tomorrow. I'll run it over and get it in."

"You don't have to."

"Relax. It's an easy fix. And I'm not doing it for you."

I nodded to show that I understood the gravity of this statement. "Sorry."

"For what?"

"Everything?"

"You think you're the center of everything, don't you?" He shook his head. "That's not what I meant. I don't mean to be rude. You just bring it out in me."

"Right. My fault then."

His lips curled in a pained expression. "Also not what I meant. Rosalind says you pull me back into the past, to the man I once was. But I'm not that person anymore."

"She knows our history?"

"I don't hide things from my wife."

"Of course. I wasn't suggesting that you did."

"I'm different now," he said. "I've changed, you know. I got saved."

"Rosalind's a lucky woman."

"She brings the best out in people. And she wants to be friends with you."

"Guess I'm lucky, too."

"Be nice. She deserves your best."

He hadn't yet mentioned the drawer I'd left open, my intrusion into their privacy.

"Is she okay? The shots." They were for infertility. I'd looked it up. "I shouldn't have snooped."

"We've lost three babies," he said softly into the damp air. "So we're trying IVF. She has faith it will work."

"I'm so sorry." This time I meant it. Something of the old sadness seeped back. It swept me into the past, and out of instinct or memory, I reached for him to soothe the pain.

He pulled back as my fingers brushed his cheek.

"Do you want to be friends with me?" I asked.

"I can't be anything with you. You know that. But I do care, Laura. And I hope she saves you, too."

He stepped around me to the stairs.

Only later did I remember my childhood church lessons. Jesus was the savior. No one else.

If Pete was misled on this point, I couldn't blame him. Rosalind was transcendent. Worship made sense when she led the songs. My favorite piece was the one with the chorus based on a psalm, about pain in the night being followed by joy in the morning. Most people stuck with the music as written and descended the scale at the end of the line, but Rosalind changed the melody so it rose several notes and opened up in crescendo. Her voice rang through the sanctuary like daybreak.

I went back to the Sunday Sisters. I nodded along at their sentiments and smiled at the stories about their children. Through these stories, I learned how to read Rosalind's face—the flinch of her eyes, the way her smile hardened.

I imagined myself her protector of sorts, redirecting conversations away from kids and deflecting questions I considered too personal. Whether she ever took note of this, I don't know, but once while I was helping her clean the kitchen, she grabbed my arm and said, "I couldn't do this without you, Laura. You just know when to step in."

She could easily have been talking about the dishes. I tried not to read into it.

Rosalind introduced me to her friend who worked as a school administrator, and soon I was on call for substitute teaching.

"The students are great," I told her, though they were not. After a year of school shutdowns, everyone was more anxious and prone to tears. No one knew how to stay in their seats. It was nice to have the work though, a reason to leave the house for something other than the pharmacy or the doctor's office. "Thank you for thinking of me."

"We're here for you," she said. Her expression was so earnest and her stature overwhelmed me.

"Me, too," I said, searching for some kind of response.

"Whatever you need, let us know. You've been such a good friend to both me and Pete. We want to support you through this difficult time."

She was the one I should have called when my mother started coughing up blood. Instead, I dialed Pete.

It was late, past midnight, but he met me in the waiting area of the emergency room. He came alone. The hospital was short-staffed and after they admitted my mother, we sat there for hours, playing the quiet game. Don't be the one to break the silence. Pete lost every round. He didn't know we were playing.

When the doctor finally came to talk to me, Pete took my hand and gave it a squeeze. He didn't let go. The doctor was extraordinarily young and overwhelmed. His fingers picked absently at the acne scars on his chin as he casually threw out terms like massive hemoptysis and therapeutic bronchoscope. More testing needed later. For now, my mother was sleeping and stable. They'd keep her overnight. I could see her if I wanted to, but he recommended that I let my husband take me home and get some rest. Pete pulled his hand away but didn't correct him.

A bright strip of light above my mother's bed staged her pale face like a lab specimen or an exhibition piece. Stone still and almost waxen under that garish light, this woman did not look like my mother. Yet there she was. Who else could she be? I touched her freckled hand, careful not to disturb the taped-down IV or otherwise jolt her out of sleep. I smoothed her hair and promised to bring her a change of clothes and Cal's Bible. I promised her more chocolate, more red wine. The machines around her beeped.

Outside, Pete paused with his hand resting on the passenger's side door. "Do you need somewhere to go?"

The sky was still muted and dark. "Nothing's open," I said.

"I know a place."

He turned left out of the parking lot, headed west on the highway. The patches of farmland were blanketed in snow. When we stopped at the woods, I couldn't recount the turns we'd made to arrive there. The trees glowed in the cold half-light of dawn.

"Where are we?"

He parked off the side of the road and pointed ahead of us. "You can see the mill from here."

"I don't see anything." Just rows of staggered trees, gray branches lined with iridescent ice. Pete cut the engine.

The snow crunched underneath our feet. Before too long, the granite slab of the building's back wall came into view. Here was the site where fifteen men had died, among them our fathers. Pete gave me his hand as I shuffled down the last embankment. He pulled back a section of broken chain-link fence and I crawled through.

"Is it safe here?" I asked when we stepped inside the mill. My voice echoed back at me.

"Stay close to the wall."

I followed him up the iron stairs and sat next to him on the landing.

"I'm not sure this is stable." But like him, I dangled my legs over the edge. We hovered above the charred walls and abandoned machinery, visitors to a great looming emptiness. "Do you come here a lot?"

"Only when I want to feel holy." Pete closed his eyes and kept them shut.

"Are you praying?" I asked.

"No." He opened his eyes.

"Will you pray for my mom?"

"I already do. Mostly, I just like to sit here."

"And feel holy."

"It's not me. It's this place. Places like this, they're blessed somehow. They're more than what they used to be. They contain more. It's like a place struck by lightning."

"Cursed, you mean."

"The presence of God is here."

I closed my eyes and tried to catch a sense of holiness, but mostly I thought of the hydraulics bursting, flames gobbling up dry pulp, smothered screaming. "Feels creepy."

"It's peaceful, if you let it be."

Our breaths made trails of smoke in the air, floating up until they dissipated into nothing.

"Want a cigarette?"

"Yeah," he said with a small laugh. "I really do."

We passed one back and forth without speaking. After putting it out, he said, "We got an embryo. All those shots for one healthy embryo. They did the genetic testing and everything. We're going to implant it next week."

"That's good. It's nice to have good news."

"It doesn't feel good, though. All I really feel is dread. I'm getting ready for another loss."

"They did the tests, though. Maybe it'll live," I said. "You'll be a father."

His face twisted, almost ugly. "Don't tease, Laura."

"Pete. I promise I'm not." Then, after a pause. "Does she know I know all this?"

He didn't answer. "We made it to sixteen weeks once. That's a lot, you know. Most people start telling others after eleven weeks, but Roz didn't. She wanted to wait till twenty weeks, even though she was already starting to show, just a little."

"That sounds wise." What else could I say?

"I wasn't home that day. Weekend job. She never called. I got home, and she was in the kitchen, just sitting in a puddle of blood. I thought she'd been stabbed or something. She'd been spotting for a day, but she didn't want to say anything. She still didn't want to go to the hospital. She looked at me as if I wasn't even there."

I tried not to see what he was saying. I willed Rosalind to get up off of that floor, to pull it together, goddamnit. Find her way back into that perfect, polished shape.

"Do you know what a fetus looks like at sixteen weeks?" He continued before I could answer. "Ours was still gift wrapped. Trapped in plastic. En caul is what they say. I could see his face, teeny tiny. He had arms and legs, wrapped around himself. The only one who would ever hold him. He looked so complete. Self-contained."

"God's love is sufficient," I intoned.

"But unto whom? What about us? Roz needs a baby. She was made to be a mom."

"She has another chance now."

Pete shook his head. "Our babies realize who their dad is and they get the hell out. Skip town before they even get here."

"Oh, Pete. Don't say that."

"It's me. I know it. The genes aren't right. You know what? I don't think I've ever wanted to be a dad. Even now. It scares the shit out of me."

"That's okay. Rosalind will be a good mom. She'll be enough."

"What were we made for, do you think?"

I didn't know if he intended to place us together again in that sentence or what it meant if he did.

"I thought I wanted to make art," I said. "Then I thought maybe it wouldn't be so bad to help others make art. To express themselves."

He shook his head. "You can't make art or anything beautiful.

It wouldn't last." He gestured out at the thick, watchful silence. "This is our legacy. We were born to it."

I understood what he meant. "Does it feel like we're cursed?"

"It's not about us, Laura. It's bigger than us."

He stood and leaned against the railing, reaching a hand out into this cavernous grave. I half expected some wispy specter to rise up and greet him, but if we were really surrounded by ghostly remains, they evaded me. I tried through an act of telepathy to pinpoint the spot where my father had died, but all I got back was more emptiness.

"Let's go." I stood as well. "This place is freaking me out."

"You don't like it?" He looked troubled.

"I'm cold. It's the coldest time of day."

We were quiet walking back. I followed after him and placed my feet into the prints he left, so it looked like only one of us had returned. In the truck, he cranked the heat to the highest setting. We sat there warming up. I must have reached for him first, because he said, "I can't, Laura. I can't." But when I tried to pull back, he held onto me. Please. Please, God, please.

He was crying when he started kissing me, slowly at first, almost innocently. Each time he paused to catch a sob, he came back hungrier, harsher. I didn't care for his trembling lips or the salty wetness of his face, but what got me what his need, how much there was of it.

When he reached for the hem my jeans, I stopped his hand. I caught his eye and shook my head, but he pulled his hand free and undid the button, yanked at my waistband. I knew that he was never this way with his wife, that he never pulled or twisted her underwear, never covered her eyes with his hands or pushed her head to the side. This made it easier to give in. I wasn't trying to supplant her or compete with her. I was fulfilling another purpose altogether.

I needed him, too. The immensity of my hunger flooded me, and I wanted so much to believe in God. I ached for some kind of grace.

We did it like teenagers. Pete made the seat fall back, and our knees and elbows dug into each other as our bodies found their way into the awkward positions meant for our younger selves. Before I could satiate whatever had opened inside me, Pete grunted and came. He fell back into the driver's seat.

When the heat of him spilled out of me, it smelled like wet leaves and something fetid, and soon the smell was inside the whole truck. He found some crumpled napkins in the back seat. My hands shook as I cleaned up. I was thinking of Rosalind. So much for protecting her. Whatever friendship I'd imagined was just that—a fantasy. I didn't know any part of her life except this piece that I had destroyed. This piece that was now mine.

Pete pulled back out on the road, making a U-turn toward the highway. I looked out at the woods for a glimpse of the ruins that lay beyond them, but the trees obscured the view.

"Laura." Pete hesitated.

"I know," I said. "I won't tell."

"She's my whole life."

I nodded and gave his knee a squeeze. Then I walked back into the empty house. I stripped the sheets from my mother's bed. A blot of the rosy red that had leaked from her lungs now stained the mattress pad. I lay down next to it. Sunlight bloomed in the sliver between the blue curtains, so bright I shielded my eyes. Another day barging in. Who invited it? I folded my hands over my belly, fingers laced into prayer.

After my mother was released from the hospital, the calendar filled with tests and scans, some necessitating long drives into the cities. A nurse came to the house to find ways to improve the living situation. She set up a bed in the living room and taught me how to inject morphine. Another doctor, new to my mother's case, tried to convince her to begin treatment. Again, the prognosis. A few more years was not worth it to her.

When Rosalind came with a meal, I accepted it with thanks but did not invite her inside.

"We're quite tired," I apologized.

"I understand. I'm thinking of you both."

She wrapped her arms around me in a hug that lingered. I wondered if she could smell him on me. Of course she couldn't, but what if my pheromones were different? Didn't nature provide any alerts?

I thought Pete would want to keep his distance, but he called on Christmas Eve — late.

"Your mom doing okay?"

"Yeah. What's up?"

He checked about the furnace, too, before he shared his news. "The test was positive. She's over the moon."

"What test? Oh." My hand fell to rest over my own abdomen.

"I don't know what I'm going to do, if it — We've been through this too many times."

"It's different, though. You've got a real chance."

"That's what terrifies me. Don't you get it? I'm going to fuck it up. I already did."

"Pete, you can't call me about these things."

"I'm not. I'm calling to tell you that we're coming over

tomorrow. Roz is bringing dinner. I was supposed to tell you earlier."

I could hear the boy in him, defiant and truculent. "Don't be a child."

"Merry Christmas, Laura. I hope you got what you wanted."

"What do you think—"

He hung up.

Hours later and still awake, I realized my period was late. Due to the stress, probably, but it was not outside the realm of possibility—a pregnancy. I was only a little past 40, nearing the end of my fertility but still capable of conception. I met Pete at 14. We'd been drawn to each other or to the same poisoned flame. Did that make us a match? Would our genes simply seek the darkness in each other?

A myth about fairness: When one person dies, another is born—my mother's nine months ticking up against the clock as my body swelled up. The Sunday Sisters would be shocked. I would never tell them it was Pete's. A mystery to last many Sunday conversations. An immaculate conception. Imagine that. Rosalind and I would sign up for prenatal yoga, compare bellies, trade books on parental folly. I'd present my miraculous bundle to my mother on her sickbed, show her something she could be proud of, something worth fighting for, but it would be too late. I'd care for the child myself. The two of us make it work somehow. We move somewhere warm and sunny. We spend weekends collaging, snipping and stitching beauty out of scraps. Like all children, mine grows up too fast. I'd be sitting at the graduation ceremony—pre-med or something equally practical, commendable—waiting for my child to walk across the stage. Maybe I'd rise with the sudden urge to pee and hurry to the bathroom, too much on my mind to be in any way prepared for the blood clotting the tissue paper, spilling onto the white tiled floor, the white bedsheets. I'd have to ask a stranger for a tampon.

"Get up," the stranger said.

My mother peered down at me, eyes owlish behind her glasses. "Apparently, we have guests coming. Pete said you knew."

I spent the afternoon cleaning. So many messes we'd made over the last few weeks. Empty pill bottles and stacks of bills. Garbage cans overflowing. I stashed away the binder with all the notes from the appointments and the nurse. At my mother's behest, I finally put the ornaments onto the tree, which we'd left bare except a string of lights. Most of the ornaments were new, but at the bottom of the box were a few I recognized from childhood. The gingerbread, the glass star, the wire angel my father made.

The door rang. Rosalind burst in with a tumult of energy. "I just knew we would have so much leftover," she said. "I wanted to put it to good use and also spend time with you lovely people. Service last night was beautiful, wasn't it? We left early though. I've got a few things to heat up. I thought it would be easier to do it here."

I watched Rosalind follow my mother into the kitchen before cornering Pete by the Christmas tree.

"I didn't make you do anything," I said, quietly. "You used me. Don't do it again."

He looked forlornly at the tree, reaching out to finger the angel ornament.

I understood then the need I once had to cut him out of my life. Even now, part of me hurt for him.

"Be better," I said, leaving him there.

In the kitchen, Rosalind had made my mother laugh, in a way I hadn't managed all these months since I'd returned home. Some story about people at the church.

"Thanks for letting us join you today," she said. Her smile seemed almost shy. "I never really knew Pete's family, you know. I've only met one aunt. It's sweet to be with you."

"He never had much family," I said. "But that's changed now."

Her eyes shined as she grasped my hand. "Pray for us," she whispered. The oven timer beeped and she turned to prepare the food. I offered to assemble a salad.

The kitchen filled with the warm smells of home and family feasts. Pete stepped in, clasping a hand over his wife's shoulder, placing a kiss near her temple. He took the glasses from her hand and carried them to the table, pouring water into each. I lit three candles for the centerpiece.

My mother sat across from Pete and I took the seat facing Rosalind. For a moment, the four of us joined hands, closing our circle. If anyone had looked in from the windows, we would have made a lovely sight, nourished and full of light.

Stories within this collection have previously appeared (at times under different titles) in the following:

"Here is the Church, Here is the Steeple," *Pank*
"Home," *Alaska Quarterly Review*
"Camp Wish-Song," *Third Coast Magazine*
"Last Night with the Brothers K," *Narrative Magazine*
"Intermission," *Gulf Coast*
"We Lived Like Astronauts," *American Chordata*
"A Visitation for the Spirit Festival," *Where the Stars Rise*, from Laksa Media
"Sweet Scoundrel," *Electric Literature*
"Joy Comes in the Morning," *The Missouri Review*

NOTES

Many of these stories lift inspiration as well as direct text from the work of others, including:

Leta Hong Fincher's *Betraying Big Brother* and Rowena He's *Tiananmen Exiles*,

Constance Garnett's translation of *The Brothers Karamazov* by Fyodor Dostoevsky,

Various translations of the writing of Zhang Ailing (Eileen Chang),

Quotes and echoes pulled from Bram Stoker's *Dracula* and Vladimir Nabokov's *Lolita*,

Paraphrased passages from Stephen Owen's meditations on memory and time in *Remembrances: The Experience of the Past in Classical Chinese Literature*

ACKNOWLEDGMENTS

Having carried a number of these stories with me for over ten years, I received help and guidance from so many people along the way. I am bowled over with gratitude.

For their early kindness and support of the shy kid: Stephen Schwandt, Mara Corey, Mrs. Yaglowski. (I didn't know your first name then, but I remembered the overwhelming pride of having my story transferred onto transparencies and projected to my captive classmates. This taught me the thrill of having a reader).

For the teachers who gave these stories their time and attention: Stuart Dybek, Anna Keesey, Sheila Donohue, Kevin Canty, Dee McNamer, and especially Debra Magpie Earling, who brought together all the witchy weird ones and taught us to listen for ghosts.

For workshop guidance and insights that helped me find the shape of certain pieces: Jess Walter, Victor LaValle, Lan Samantha Chang, Marlon James.

For the manuscript shuffles and thoughtful notes: John Englehardt, Jordan Rossen.

For story-inspiring quotes and conversation: BC Oliva, Caitlin Stainken Buhl, Virginia Zech, Maud Streep.

For the many people who have exchanged work with me at the University of Montana, Hugo House, and the Loft Literary Center.

For the editors who sought to bring out the best in their selections: Laura Jok, Evelyn Somers, Ariel Berry, Mimi Kusch, and Halimah Marcus.

For my publisher, YesYes Books, and KMA Sullivan for the number of reviews and conversations.

For the institutions that offered me the time and resources to hide out and indulge my inner hermit: Hedgebrook, The M Literary Residency, Artist Trust of Washington State, and the Sitka Center for Art and Ecology.

And for those who kept me from total isolation: Elizabeth De Souza, Heidi Durrow, Roja Heydarpour, Jael Humphrey, Wendy Johnson, Michelle Ruiz Keil, and Julie Phillips. Also: Juan and Deng, who came to bust ghosts.

For my Seattle writing community: Katie Ellison, Paul Hlava Ceballos, Alex Gallo-Brown, Joyce Chen, Bretty Rawson, Lisa Chen, Daniel Tam-Claiborne, Bill Carty, Jane Wong, Josh Fomon, Courtney Bird, JP Kemmick, Ching-In Chen, Juan Carlos Reyes, Katie Prince, Lindsay Hood.

For affirming to me what big dreams and consistent action can do: Rosanna Sze, JM Wong, Shuxuan Zhou.

For all the ones who have stood by me and whispered *brave*.

For my mother and sister, for walking ahead of me.

For Nancy, Darcie, and Lara—bonus mothers and sisters.

For the rest of my family and their unwavering support.

Finally, for Bion, for walking next to me, every direction all the time.

Born in the Hebei province of China and raised in the American Midwest, DIANA XIN's work appears in *Electric Literature*, *Narrative Magazine*, *Gulf Coast*, *The Missouri Review*, and elsewhere. She studied creative writing at the University of Montana and is a recipient of residencies from Hedgebrook, the M Literary Residency in Beijing, and the Sitka Center for Art and Ecology. *Book of Exemplary Women* (YesYes Books, 2025) is her debut collection of short stories. She resides in Seattle, Washington.

ALSO BY YESYES BOOKS

FICTION
The Nothing by Lauren Davis
Girls Like Me by Nina Packebush
Three Queerdos and a Baby by Nina Packebush

WRITING RESOURCES
Gathering Voices: Creating a Community-Based Poetry Workshop
by Marty McConnell

FULL-LENGTH POETRY COLLECTIONS
Ugly Music by Diannely Antigua
Bone Language by Jamaica Baldwin
Cataloguing Pain by Allison Blevins
Strange Flowers by Bryan Byrdlong
What Runs Over by Kayleb Rae Candrilli
Don't Cut Your Own Bangs by Caroline Crew
This, Sisyphus by Brandon Courtney
Salt Body Shimmer by Aricka Foreman
Gutter by Lauren Brazeal Garza
Forever War by Kate Gaskin
Inconsolable Objects by Nancy Miller Gomez
Ceremony of Sand by Rodney Gomez
Undoll by Tanya Grae
Loudest When Startled by luna rey hall

Everything Breaking / For Good by Matt Hart
Brine Orchid by Arah Ko
40 WEEKS by Julia Kolchinsky
murmurations by Anthony Thomas Lombardi
Sons of Achilles by Nabila Lovelace
Refusenik by Lynn Melnick
GOOD MORNING AMERICA I AM HUNGRY AND ON FIRE
     by jamie mortara
Born Backwards by Tanya Olson
a falling knife has no handle by Emily O'Neill
To Love An Island by Ana Portnoy Brimmer
Another Way to Split Water by Alycia Pirmohamed
Tell This to the Universe by Katie Prince
One God at a Time by Meghan Privitello
I'm So Fine: A List of Famous Men & What I Had On
     by Khadijah Queen
If the Future Is a Fetish by Sarah Sgro
Gilt by Raena Shirali
[insert] boy by Danez Smith
Say It Hurts by Lisa Summe
Hand Over Hand Over the Edge of the World by Patrick Swaney
Boat Burned by Kelly Grace Thomas
Helen Or My Hunger by Gale Marie Thompson
As She Appears by Shelley Wong

RECENT CHAPBOOK COLLECTIONS
Vinyl 45s
     Exit Pastoral by Aidan Forster
     Crown for the Girl Inside by Lisa Low
     Phantasmagossip by Sara Mae

The Year of the Sheep by Stacey Park
Scavenger by Jessica Lynn Suchon
Unmonstrous by John Allen Taylor
Giantess by Emily Vizzo

Blue Note Editions
Kissing Caskets by Mahogany L. Browne
One Above One Below: Positions & Lamentations by Gala
Mukomolova
The Porch (As Sanctuary) by Jae Nichelle